AGE IS JUST A
NUMBER

AGE IS JUST A NUMBER

To an enduring friendship!

Myrliss

Myrliss Hershey

To order additional copies of this book, contact:
Xlibris Corporation
1-888-795-4274
www.Xlibris.com
Orders@Xlibris.com
53145

To My Family

CHAPTER ONE

While the driver stacked her luggage on the sidewalk, Marvela reached back into the taxi to retrieve her cane. She tipped him, then turned and stood looking at the imposing three-story brick building. Marvela looked for a long time, up and down and across the building, taking it all in and comparing it to the marketing pictures that had been sent to her with the mailing, and were, in addition, available on a Web site that showed 360-degree pictures of her new home. It was late August, but the grass was lush and green, yet not quite as perfectly cut, and thick, and as green as she saw in the pictures.

Colorful beds of impatiens bordered the walkways. Hostas, some of them with purple flowers on top of thin spires, hugged the shade of the building. Glancing at her five large and mismatched suitcases, Marvela felt overwhelmed and apprehensive. She hesitated before entering. A smiling, young, plump (the kind of young woman who had never been really thin) receptionist greeted her.

"May I help you?"

"Yes," she smiled back. "My name is Marvela Higglesford. I have rented apartment 303 in Independent Living. My furniture should have arrived yesterday. I will need help with the luggage on the sidewalk outside."

"It will take a few minutes. I'll have to call one of the maintenance men. In the meantime, I can give you the key to your apartment, and you can have a look around—the elevators are to your left." She handed Marvela a set of keys and answered the phone, which had been ringing throughout their conversation with an irritating ring that was much too loud for a reception area.

Marvela placed the keys in the outside pocket of her bulging purse, threw it over one shoulder, grabbed her cane and made her way to the elevators. She looked around the empty lobby. Tastefully decorated, it was the first floor of an atrium that featured railed balconies and lots of greenery (but perhaps, a bit fake looking—were they silk?) in corner planters.

So far, she was pleased with the look of things. She had chosen *Forest Glen* after researching dozens of retirement homes on the Internet. She'd ordered brochures from the top six. After careful study, Marvela chose three of them to investigate more thoroughly. *Forest Glen* was the most expensive of the three, but it offered amenities that pleased her. It had a heated indoor swimming pool and a Jacuzzi. There was state-of-the-art exercise equipment, and the services of a trainer. Continental breakfasts were complimentary, and she could choose to eat lunch or dinner. Fresh fruit was always available in the dining room. Marvela spoke on the phone to the marketing director numerous times, and felt she was well-informed on all of the details.

Marvela chose the location in Johnson County, Kansas, because it was midway between her two sons who lived in the States—Steve, the oldest, and more outgoing one, in Philadelphia, and Ron, tall and thin, with much too long hair, in San Francisco. Also, she would have fairly easy access to an international airport outside of Kansas City, Missouri. Her daughter, Marie, the youngest, lived in England; she hoped to visit her occasionally. Marvela chose not to visit the retirement community before moving, preferring to save airfare from New York, and applying it to the considerable expense of moving her furniture.

Marvela had lived for the past thirty years in a rent-controlled apartment in New York City, which was very large, and had tall, wide windows that went to the floor. The apartment in *Forest Glen* was considerably smaller, (about nine hundred square feet) and darker.

She was forced to sell or give away a lot of furniture. Even so, she had kept more furniture than the new apartment would easily accommodate; Marvela possessed family antiques she could not bring herself to sell, nor, at this point, distribute among her children.

Marvela fumbled in her purse for the key after she found her apartment. It took her several tries to open the door. She caught her breath. Marvela thought at first that her place had been ransacked as all the furniture and items were in disarray and boxes were stacked. Some had even fallen over.

She had sent the moving company diagrams of the rooms, carefully marking where each piece should be placed. The beds for the two bedrooms were in pieces in the living room, and the living room furniture had been randomly placed in the bedrooms. Marvela hoped the maintenance people would be available to move the heavy pieces, and set things right.

There was a telephone on the floor. Thank goodness it was working. She found the number for the marketing director, who had assured her there would be help available. Unfortunately the director was out. She tried the main number for Forest Glen. After over twenty rings the receptionist answered, "*Forest Glen*, may I help you?" Marvela told her of the need to have help moving furniture.

"I'll make out a work order, ma'am, and someone will get to you as soon as possible. Unfortunately our maintenance staff is a bit shorthanded today; two of the men called in sick."

"It is nearly five o'clock, and I haven't eaten since breakfast," Marvela said a bit impatiently. "Is it too late to make reservations for dinner? "Also, if I don't get help setting up my bed, I'll have no place to sleep tonight."

"I understand, ma'am, we'll do the best we can. I'll give you the extension for the dining room."

Marvela was able to make a reservation for dinner at five thirty, so she rushed to get cleaned up as best she could, since her suitcases hadn't arrived. She washed her face, fixed her makeup from the supplies she carried in her purse, and went in search of the dining room. She met a very wrinkled and white-haired woman in the hall, introduced herself, and asked directions. Betty, who was in a wheelchair, told her the dining room was on the second floor, left of the elevators.

"You must be new. I just came from eating. The food was pretty good tonight." Marvela was a bit taken back that people in wheelchairs were allowed in Independent Living. She also wondered about the statement that the food was good *tonight.* She had been assured that the food was always of the highest quality.

When Marvela got to the dining room, she looked around as she waited to be seated. She was impressed by the decor. Fresh flowers graced each white-damask-covered table. The tables were set for two, four, or six. Greenery filled planters added an outdoor feeling to the place. The majority of the diners were women, mostly older than herself; but men seemed to make up a sizable minority. She was seated at a table with three women and handed a black faux leather menu. A variety of entrees, side dishes, and desserts were featured.

The servers, who looked like high school or college students, were dressed in black pants, white shirts, and black ties. Marvela introduced herself to her tablemates and discovered she would be dining with three widows. Florence May, overweight but attractive, had been a doctor's wife. Mary Vasser, a frail-looking woman in a wheelchair, had been university professor's wife.

Edith Smithson, the youngest of the three, had been a lawyer's wife.

During the course of the conversation, they revealed that each had given up a career to be full-time housewives and mothers. Marvela told them she was a divorcee who had worked as a magazine editor and television producer while her children were growing up.

"That must have been difficult," Florence said sympathetically.

"Yes, it was, but I was fortunate to find good day care, and my children went to good schools . . . that is after a few bad starts," Marvela smiled.

"*Forest Glen* is a long ways from New York. How did you find this place?" Mary asked.

"I was looking for a retirement community equidistant from my two sons. The oldest one, Steve, lives in Philadelphia, and the younger one, Ron, lives in San Francisco. I also needed to be near an international airport. My daughter, Marie, lives in London," Marvela replied.

"You didn't want to live with your children?" Edith asked, grinning.

"I take it you didn't take that option either," Marvela said as she looked at the laughing women.

"My kids are great," Florence commented, "but I want to remain their friend."

"I did consider finding a place near my daughter, but I wasn't ready to live in London, Besides I would have been too far from my sons," Marvela said shaking her head.

"Do you have grandchildren?" Mary queried.

"I have two little ones, children of my son, Steve, and his second wife. Ron, the one who lives in San Francisco, had a brief marriage that didn't work out. My daughter is engaged to be married." Marvela appreciated the women's interest, but felt she had revealed enough about her family, so she asked the women about their lives.

Mary didn't have children; she confided her husband was sterile. Florence had six children and fourteen grandchildren.

"Most of them live in Kansas and Missouri, so I have many visitors, for which I'm very thankful. Most of the grandchildren are grown now. One is married, so I may be a great-grandmother soon," she said proudly.

Edith hesitated before she spoke. "I've had only two letters from my only son this last year. He asked for money in both of them. He has been in and out of rehabilitation for drug addiction." She had tears in her eyes.

Marvela was surprised at the revelations the women shared so willingly. She wondered if such open sharing was customary in this part of the country, or if it was typical of most retirement communities.

Edith asked if she played bridge.

"I was always too busy to learn, and I guess I wasn't too interested," Marvela replied.

After a rather strained silence, Edith said, "Bridge keeps me sane—that, plus good books, and DVDs."

Marvela brightened. "Oh, I love to read. I understand we also have access to free continuing education classes at the university."

"I haven't enrolled in any classes. I guess I had enough of university life when my husband was alive," Mary said, shrugging her shoulders.

"What kind of books do you like to read?" Marvela queried with interest.

"Mostly mysteries," Edith replied, "and you?"

"I favor historical novels and books that feature other cultures. Lately I've been enjoying biographies of successful contemporary women." Marvela replied. Noting the women weren't impressed, she changed the subject. "Are any of you taking aqua aerobics classes?"

The three women shook their heads. "I sometimes go to the Fit for Life classes, mostly stretching while seated," Mary offered. "Aqua aerobics would probably be good for me, but there isn't wheelchair access to the swimming pool."

"There's also no readily available help for those of us who are dependent on walkers," Edith motioned to a row of walkers next to the wall. Marvela nodded and looked around. She noted several people leaving the room using walkers and canes; only three or four walked without help. Most of the people she saw seemed to be in their eighties, maybe even nineties, older than she anticipated. But it wasn't always easy to judge ages. She was seventy-four, and most of her friends and former colleagues in New York were younger.

Surely she'd find some residents here who would be interested in some of the things she liked. She had glanced at the activities schedule on the bulletin board by the receptionist's desk and noted that a writing group met weekly. She'd have to look into that. She also noted that a "block party" was to be held the next day for residents on her floor. The receptionist told her that block parties were held monthly on the various floors to facilitate getting acquainted with neighbors.

When she got back to her apartment, she found her suitcases in the hallway. But nothing had been done about her furniture. She waited until ten that night before getting ready for bed, then rummaged among the boxes until she found some sheets, a pillow, and a blanket. She made a makeshift bed on the sofa. Unable to sleep, she reviewed events of the day. Thankfully the nonstop flight from New York to the Kansas City Airport was uneventful, and on time. She was also grateful that it didn't seem as hot and dry as she had been forewarned, although that would undoubtedly change. *Forest Glen* appeared to live up to its promise, but she knew it would take time to adjust to the new milieu. New York had been her home for so long. Marvela loved the city, and really wasn't emotionally prepared to leave, although her logical mind knew it was the right decision. She finally drifted into a fitful sleep.

She woke up at 6:30AM, shook out some wrinkled clothes, and dressed. She went to the dining room for breakfast around 7:00 AM. only to be told that breakfast wouldn't be served until 8:00 AM. Feeling frustrated and desperate for a cup of coffee, she sorted through several boxes until she found her coffeemaker and a half-empty sack of coffee. She unpacked a box of plates, and started on a second box before she found a cup.

Marking the boxes *China* just didn't cut it. Although she preferred half-and-half in her coffee, black had to be OK for now. She dragged a chair out on the balcony and sipped the stimulating liquid. The morning was fairly cool. Other than birdsongs, it was very quiet. She felt better after the cup of fresh brew, but her stomach was growling. She had hardly touched the airplane food the day before. Glancing at her watch, she saw it was past eight, so she went to the dining room in search of food.

Looking around for coffee, she noted that a coffee dispenser labeled "regular" was sitting on a table where five men were watching her with interest.

"Most people want decaf, but we drink regular, so we keep it here," one of the men explained.

"We're the 'regulars.' Feel free to help yourself." The rotund man chuckled and offered to fill her cup.

They asked her name and introduced themselves: Larry, Amos, Gabriel, Jack, and Dave.

"It's self-service here at breakfast," Gabriel said smiling. His halo of white hair gave him a resemblance to his heavenly namesake. Their ages probably ranged from seventy something to ninety or more.

Marvela helped herself to the breakfast bar and found an empty table. The men at the nearby table were joking and laughing—a welcome contrast to the rather somber tone of the dining room at dinner. She returned to her apartment after breakfast, and waited about two hours before the head maintenance man showed up to look things over. An hour later, three men came to move the furniture.

"This is above and beyond our maintenance duties, ma'am, so we'll have to charge you for this service," the foreman explained.

Marvela was disappointed, but told them to put it on her bill. As she began to empty the contents of the boxes, she mentally added up her first impressions of *Forest Glen*.

On the plus side, it was nicely decorated and clean. On the minus side, she felt no effort had been made to welcome her as a newcomer, or to acquaint her with the schedule or logistics. She was also somewhat taken aback by the handicaps most of the residents evidenced. It was a contrast to the glossy promotion brochures, which depicted healthy people playing golf and enjoying the pool. She reminded herself not to jump to hasty conclusions.

A ringing telephone interrupted her reverie. It was Jan, the marketing director. "I see you got here on schedule. Is there anything we can do for you?"

"I may need help hanging pictures and moving some furniture," Marvela replied. "Is there a charge for that?"

"The maintenance people are supposed to help with some of that, within reason of course."

"Evidently moving furniture that was unloaded quite haphazardly is not within reason," Marvela said with a touch of sarcasm.

"That is quite possible, but I'll check with maintenance to see what I can do," Jan replied cheerfully. "By the way, could you come down today and complete your paperwork?"

Jan was certainly a marketing plus for *Forest Glen*. She was decidedly efficient and always pleasant and friendly. She made one feel looked after. Marvela wasn't sure the rest of the staff was that competent.

After Marvela completed the paperwork, she noted the fees came to more than she had anticipated. Not surprisingly, they had increased since she got the first estimates.

She had the funds, but feared that eventually the payments would begin to deplete the inheritance she hoped to leave her children. She also wanted to buy a car. She hadn't needed one in New York, but felt it would be useful here. Bus service was offered as part of the rent package, but she felt the need to be more independent.

Marvela passed the library on the way to her apartment and noticed three women munching on rolls. She remembered the notice about the block party. Surely there were more residents than that on this floor. She estimated at least twenty, possibly more. The women beckoned to her to join them. Two were in wheelchairs.

"Come join us. We'd like to welcome you to our floor." Marvela recognized the speaker as Betty, the woman who gave her directions to the dining room.

"Thank you. I'll stop by for a few minutes to get acquainted, but I'm in the midst of trying to get settled in my apartment," Marvela replied as she joined the women.

The other two introduced themselves as Ruth and Frances.

"I believe I live next door to you," Ruth said smiling at Marvela. "If you have questions about the place, feel free to ask. I've lived here for five years, so I pretty well know the ropes."

"Ruth has just been elected secretary of our newly formed residents' advisory committee," Frances informed her. "She will take any complaints you have to the committee, not that it will do a lot of good," she added with a touch of bitterness. Marvela was a bit taken aback. "What are some of your complaints?"

"Well, for one, there is little or no adaptation in our apartments for wheelchair residents. Also the bussing fees have been raised. I don't think we get our money's worth around here." Frances frowned. Betty nodded her head.

"It's actually a pretty nice place," Ruth interjected. "Wheelchair residents do have some legitimate complaints, but I'm told the management is working on some solutions."

"I guess there isn't a community that doesn't have problems to work out. I'll reserve judgment until I know the place better," Marvela remarked in an attempt to be conciliatory. "I'd better get back to my apartment, there's so much to do." She shook hands with the women. "I'll be in touch," she said as she left the room.

She wondered if block parties attracted the complainers. Maybe that was one reason the attendance was so poor.

CHAPTER TWO

A priority at this time was the need to go grocery shopping. Marvela was on her own for lunches, and her larder was bare. She called the front desk and inquired about the bus schedule.

"There won't be a grocery run until tomorrow morning, but you can book a van for a fee of five dollars."

Marvela sighed, "In that case, please schedule a van for me as soon as possible."

"That will be about one o'clock. Please be in the lobby."

Marvela looked around the apartment, dismayed by the many boxes to be emptied. She decided to start tackling the challenging task until it was time to meet the van. She had unpacked three boxes, contents scattered on the floor, when the receptionist called. The jovial driver met her in the lobby. During the nine-block drive to the nearest grocery store, he kept up a constant chatter, filling her in on some of the history of the area.

"*Forest Glen* is located in a fairly new development in Johnson County, Kansas, a suburb of Kansas City Missouri."

"So are we still in Kansas?"

"We're about eight blocks from State Street, the dividing line between Missouri and Kansas. We aren't far from the famous Plaza shopping area. It has a dozen or more beautiful fountains. You won't want to miss seeing the Plaza at Christmas when all of the buildings are lit. It's quite a sight," the driver enthused.

At the grocery store, Marvela bought some sandwich fixings for her lunches. She picked up whole grain bread, cans of tuna, pickle relishes, vegetable juice, apples, sliced cheese, and baby carrots. When she got to her apartment, she fixed a tuna salad sandwich, and ate her lunch while reading the local paper, which had been left on her doorstep. She perused it, but found little that interested her. While crossing the lobby she'd noticed the *New York Times* on one of the tables. There was a sign stating it was not to be removed from the lobby. She would go down later and read her favorite newspaper.

The boxes beckoned, but she decided to take a short nap. She slept soundly until five thirty when she awoke with a start. It was dinnertime, and she hadn't ironed any clothes to wear. She went through the clothes in two suitcases before she found a seersucker pantsuit that looked fairly decent. She dressed hastily, freshened her makeup, and rushed to dinner. The dining room was almost empty by the time she got there, so she chose to sit by herself. It would be difficult to become accustomed to such early dinner hours. As she read the menu, she discovered the selection wasn't as varied as the night before, but the food was served hot, and it was tasty.

When she got back to her apartment, she glanced at the boxes and opened a few. But the task seemed daunting, so she took a hot shower, found some sheets, and made up her bed. She read until she fell asleep. In her dreams she was still in New York, packing for the trip. When it was time to leave, she was unable to find her makeup, so she had to go to the airport shiny faced and pale, not even a lipstick in her purse.

When she woke up, she smiled as she recalled her dream. She had to admit to a bit of vanity. Examining herself in the full-length mirror, she recalled some friends telling her she didn't look a day over sixty. Well, that was an exaggeration from friends who liked to flatter her, but thanks to a few nips and tucks, and judicious use of cosmetics, she might pass for ten years younger than her real age of seventy-four—provided the lighting was very dim.

She brushed her short naturally wavy hair, a chosen ash-blonde. She had given some thought to allowing her hair to revert to its natural color. She was a natural blonde, but started coloring her hair after the birth of her first child, when it turned dull and mousy looking. It was undoubtedly gray by now, but she couldn't bring herself to make the change yet. If she remembered to straighten her shoulders and suck in her stomach, her five-foot-four figure was still fairly youthful looking, although thicker in the waist than it used to be. She had lost at least over an inch of height over the years, and hoped getting back to yoga and stretching would prohibit more loss of height. Most of her clothes were a size eight, but she was concerned that some of them were getting a bit tight. She vowed to lose some pounds and get back to regular exercise. The exercise would also help her meet the goal of getting rid of her cane.

Marvela had worked full time until she was seventy. At that time she chose to work only three days a week. This schedule suited her well for four years. She had a fulfilling life during those years. Since she worked fewer hours she had more time to attend concerts and the theater, as well as being able to assuage her guilt by visiting her Aunt

Sylvia more often. When Marvela visited her at the nursing home in New Jersey, they often reminisced about Marvela's early days in New York. Sylvia reminded Marvela of her reclusive days when she first came to New York.

"They were tough times," Marvela admitted, "but thanks to you, I overcame them, and found a lot of happiness."

"It was tough going for a while after your parents were killed. They were wonderful people. My mother also died young. Your mother, Alma, was like a second mother to me." Sylvia wiped a tear.

Marvela took Sylvia's hand. "You have been like a second mother to me, Sylvia, or maybe I should say big sister, since you are only fifteen years older than I."

Marvela graduated from Syracuse University, with a major in journalism and a minor in drama when she was twenty-one. She was born and reared in the small town of Hubbardsville, New York, a short distance from Syracuse. Her father had owned a hardware store there. She worked in the store weekends through high school and college.

After graduating from college, she obtained a job as a news reporter for the *Syracuse Post Standard*. She was looking forward to spending weekends and holidays with her parents. An only child, she was devoted to her parents. They weren't exactly pals, but she considered them wise mentors and good friends.

When her parents were killed in an automobile accident soon after she obtained her reporting position, she was devastated by the loss. She tried to continue at her reporting job, but found it difficult to cope with her overwhelming grief and devote the time and concentration the position required. Although the editors were willing to give her some time off to recover, she decided to resign. Sylvia asked her to come to New York and live with her. Marvela had some misgivings about moving to the big city, but she loved and admired her aunt. It was the best option she had. It took her nearly a month to settle her parents' estate; she wasn't motivated to move rapidly.

In New York, she was pretty much a recluse for several weeks, spending most of her time reading, in addition to cleaning and cooking for Sylvia who was employed as an assistant editor at a publishing company. Sylvia worked long hours and appreciated Marvela's help, but she was concerned about her apathy. Marvela rarely left the apartment except for venturing to a nearby grocery store and deli, and occasionally going to a movie with Sylvia.

Sylvia tried to be patient and give Marvela time to heal, but decided she needed to be more aggressive in urging her to get out more.

"Marvela, I really appreciate all you do around here, but the life of a recluse is not for you," Sylvia admonished her. "You are by nature a social being, bright, and vivacious. For my sake would you try to find something that would get you out of this apartment?"

Marvela knew Sylvia was right, so she started seriously looking over the help wanted ads. She finally took a job as a temporary office worker, while she looked for something more permanent. She felt better once she got out in the city and met people. Gregarious by nature, interaction with the people at work was good therapy.

Marvela married John, an assistant professor at New York University, a year after she came to New York City. They met at a Christmas party for faculty and their guests at the university. Sylvia had been invited by a faculty friend, and she asked if Marvela could come as well.

Marvela protested that she didn't have the right clothes. Her staple was a good black suit to which she added variety by changing blouses and scarves. Black suited her somber mood, and it was fashionable in New York. Sylvia took her shopping for a party dress, insisting she pick something colorful.

When the two went shopping, Marvela tried on a silk turquoise dress with cap sleeves, intricate straps in back, and a full skirt. She admitted it was beautiful, but much too pricey. However, Sylvia insisted on paying for it.

"Sylvia, do you remember buying me that lovely turquoise dress?" Marvela asked as she bent over to kiss her frail aunt who just woke up from a short nap.

"I'll never forget that dress. When you twirled the skirt in front of the mirror, you almost looked happy. It was well worth the price." Sylvia smiled in remembrance.

"It turned out to be a fortuitous purchase, you know. John had his eyes on me the moment I stepped into the room at the faculty party. He said turquoise was his favorite color."

"You had some good years with John, didn't you?" Sylvia asked, frowning a bit.

"Oh yes, I guess you could say we had a whirlwind courtship, and the first years of marriage were great. John was so good to me then, and we shared similar values. Would you believe we were both virgins when we married?" Marvela chuckled.

"We spent a lot of time watching videos—cheap entertainment. There were nights I was too tired to go back to your apartment so I slept on the lumpy couch."

"You were good about calling me, but I assumed you were sleeping with John," Sylvia said with a wry grin.

Marvela laughed. "One night when I stayed over, John proposed. He said we could economize by sharing an apartment. He also expressed doubts that he could 'keep me an honest woman much longer.'"

"Times were different then, couples rarely lived together openly," Sylvia said as she smiled fondly at Marvela. "John was an Ohio farm boy, wasn't he?" she asked.

"He was an only child of dairy farmers. His dad had dreams of him taking over the farm, but his mother, a college graduate, encouraged his academic career. Fortunately Stella liked me. She insisted that I have her mother's diamond solitaire as an engagement ring.

"That was a generous offer," Marvela smiled remembering Stella. "John's father wasn't in very good health, so they had a difficult time making ends meet, but they didn't talk about it."

Marvela took Sylvia's hand and kissed it. "Thanks to your financial help, I was able to fix up our apartment after we married. I replaced our old worn-out couch with a new hide-a-bed. Bargain basement curtains and bright pillows completed the makeover. John was impressed."

The time Marvela spent with Sylvia at the nursing home was rewarding in many ways. As they reminisced, she was able to put to rest some misgivings that still haunted her.

"These visits have been good for me," Marvela told her aunt. "I will never be certain I made the right decision when I divorced John and fought for custody of the children, but I don't think I could have left New York at that time."

"I don't think you could have, Marvela," Sylvia said. "Your career really took off after you divorced."

Marvela didn't work as a temp very long. Thanks to Sylvia's connections in the publishing world, she was offered a position as an editorial assistant at a major news magazine. Her work was lauded, and she was in line for an editor's position when she found she was pregnant. She was granted a month's maternity leave, not common in those days, but the editor's position was given to a man. Thirteen months later, she was devastated to learn she was pregnant again. Once more fortune smiled on her, for she was granted another month's maternity leave. Those were hectic days. Marvela's hands were reddened from washing and bleaching diapers, and mixing formula. She wasn't able to breast-feed, and there were no readily available disposable diapers at that time. The couple loved their sons, despite the work. After their chores were completed, and the babies were asleep, they often tiptoed into the makeshift nursery, and held hands as they admired their cherubic sons. John helped around the house, and was always good with the children. However, when Marvela returned to work he had trouble accepting her demanding career. Marvela was devoted to her children, and did her share of tending to their needs when she got home from work, but they were both perpetually exhausted. Their sex life suffered, and the marriage suffered with it.

Three years later, six months after Marvela had been promoted to an editor's position, Marie was born. Because her work was valued, Marvela was allowed to stay home with her daughter for three months. She performed many of her editorial tasks at home. This helped the marriage considerably. The couple managed to maintain a fairly stable married life during that time.

Shortly after Marvela returned to work, John again resented Marvela's absorption in her career. He also became unhappy with his position. He had obtained tenure, but didn't receive the promotion he expected, so he sent his curriculum vitae to other universities. He accepted a position as professor of psychology at Kansas University in Lawrence. The couple had many arguments over this decision, and there was considerable tension in the household; both were concerned about the effect on the children. Finally, John gave Marvela an ultimatum.

"Come with me, or I'll take the children and go without you."

Marvela simply couldn't envision life in a small Kansas town. She loved her job and was not ready to give it up. She was torn. She dearly loved the children and still had feelings for John. But she couldn't bring herself to leave New York. Costly custody battles ensued, which Marvela eventually won, thanks to financial help from Sylvia. The breakup was definitely not friendly. John thought Marvela was being very selfish and chided her for putting her interests ahead of the children's.

Marvela threw herself into her work after the divorce. The magazine flourished, and she was given a substantial raise in salary. She often mingled with a number of influential people in the media. When she heard of a vacancy in the news department at ABC, she applied for the job. A weekly news documentary was making its debut, and she liked the idea of working in television. She was hired as an assistant producer in charge of booking featured interviews.

Marvela exuded charm on the telephone, and had a way of subtly persuading reluctant candidates to appear on the show. She was promoted to producer after two years on the job. In this role, she traveled to many of the sites visited by various news reporters. Her all-time favorite was the interview she helped arrange with King Hussein and Queen Noor of Jordan. She corresponded with Queen Noor for several years and follows the Queen's activities with great interest to this day.

CHAPTER THREE

Marvela was lost in daydreaming as she unpacked boxes. She thought about how reluctantly she had retired from her television job. Working part-time had been perfect, but her children thought it was time for her to take it easy. True—she was tired of the commuting. It took about an hour to get to work. Also her retirement gave her the opportunity to be at Sylvia's bedside when she died. Marvela held Sylvia's hand as she peacefully slipped away at age ninety. Marvela doubted if she would have left New York had she not slipped on the ice outside her apartment on her way to the grocery store. She broke her kneecap, and was on crutches for six weeks. Her friends were very helpful, but she realized it was time for her to look for a safer environment. So here she was, and she was determined to make the best of it.

Marvela wondered if John still lived in Lawrence, about forty-five miles from *Forest Glen*. She had visited Lawrence when Marie attended KU, but had since lost track of John. Marie had his address; should she try to contact him? Just then the phone rang. It was Marie.

"Mom, are you OK?"

"Yes, dear, I'm getting settled here. I still have a lot of straightening up to do, and pictures to hang, but everything arrived safely, and I'm fine."

"Do you like *Forest Glen?*"

"So far, so good. I have mixed first impressions, but the place is lovely. I plan to take a walk this afternoon and explore the area."

"Are you feeling all right? How's the leg?"

"I've almost caught up on my sleep, and the leg is functioning quite well. Hopefully, I can get rid of the cane soon."

"Remember, if you don't like it there, we'll find something in London. Nigel sends his love. We're house hunting now. The places we like are very expensive, but we may sell our souls for a house. Both of us are tired of apartment living."

"Keep me informed. I really wish I could help you financially. By the way, do you have your father's latest address? Do you know if he's still in Lawrence?"

"He recently moved to a retirement community there. I'll e-mail his address. Now that you're so close, you should look him up. Since his wife died last year he's been very lonely. Unfortunately Steve and Ron don't stay in touch with him," Marie said ruefully.

"I'll think about calling him, but don't count on it. There's been so much water over the bridge," Marvela sighed. They talked for about twenty more minutes. Marie chattered excitedly about her upcoming marriage and the vagaries of house hunting.

"This call will cost you a fortune, Marie, but I loved every minute of it. I'll e-mail you later today and give you more details. My computer isn't set up, but they have a computer room for residents here. Take good care, I love you."

"Love you too, Mom. We'll be in touch."

After hanging up, Marvela allowed herself to shed a few tears. She missed Marie so very much. Marie was a mother's pride and joy, almost too good to be true. Marvela admired her for staying in close touch with her father. Steve and Ron's relationship with John was strained. They were more affected by the divorce than their sister was and blamed their dad for leaving the family, even though Marvela explained to them she was largely to blame for not going with him when he moved to Kansas. Marie lived with Marvela in New York for several years after she graduated as a drama major from Kansas University in Lawrence. While in New York, she attended countless auditions. When she landed a starring role in an off-Broadway production, she felt she was on her way to making it in New York; but the breaks didn't come her way. She soon became tired of understudy roles, and eventually became weary of the New York scene. Marvela had some theater contacts in London. She had briefly dated a British television producer whose brother made a name for himself directing *Cats* in London. Marvela also used her business contacts to help get Marie a job as a secretary at the British Broadcasting Company in London.

Marie continued her summer visits to her father until she went to England. The boys stopped their summer visits when they were in high school and had summer jobs. Marvela spoke to her thirty-four-year-old daughter by phone at least twice a week, and e-mailed her almost daily. She e-mailed Steve and Ron weekly, but heard from them once or twice a month. Steve was a successful lawyer, and his lifestyle was harried. His second wife was a younger woman who had her own career as a design consultant. They had two preschool children who kept them busy. Marvela was reminded of her early parenting days. Ron lived in a one-room studio in San Francisco. He was a CEO of a nonprofit political organization, a role he loved, but he was always short of money. Marie seemed to have liked John's second wife, although she didn't talk much about her. Elaine chose to be a full-time housewife, and seemed to take good care of John. There was no doubt John would feel lost without her.

Marvela had last seen John at Marie's college graduation. She had gone to dinner with Elaine and John, along with Marie and some of her friends. Marvela found some old picture albums and paged through them until she found a picture of the group at a restaurant. John was still handsome then, though prematurely gray. Lovely brunette Marie had her arms around both parents. John's rather plain-looking wife, Elaine, had put her hand possessively on John's arm, and wore a forced smile. Marvela looked quite glamorous. She just had her teeth whitened, and she smiled dazzlingly at the camera.

Marvela laid the album on the table and closed her eyes. She tried to analyze her feelings. At the time the picture was taken, she was still somewhat attracted to John, and remembered feeling some jealousy about the seeming success of his second marriage.

She wondered how John had aged. He was always an exercise freak, so he probably kept close to his ideal weight. Marvela put away the picture album and spent the next few hours sorting clothes. There wasn't enough closet space for her wardrobe, so she had to decide what to put in storage. She hung up her summer clothes and a few fall things. There would be little need for her dressy clothes here. Casual seemed to be the fashion mode. She had even noted sweats and housedress-looking attire on some of the residents. She wondered if people in this part of the country dressed up for the theater. She knew she would. She had too many nice clothes not to wear them when she went out.

Marvela had dinner with a friendly couple who filled her in on things she should know about *Forest Glen*. She wasn't surprised to hear the average age was around eighty-three. No wonder so many residents needed help to walk. After dinner she went to the front desk to pick up a calendar of events and a telephone book. She also picked up a key to her storage area. It was disappointedly small, and she wondered where she would store her extra clothes—probably under the bed.

As she read over the calendar, she saw several events that interested her. There was bus service to shows at the outdoor Starlight Theater in Kansas City. Marie had attended many of the performances when she lived in Lawrence, and thought they were quite good. Marvela decided to sign up for the remaining summer show. There were also some interesting-sounding programs at *Forest Glen*, including the regularly scheduled writing group. She was pleased to find there were such activities available, and penciled them on her calendar.

She first attended the writing group as an observer. Ten members were present; four men and six women. Their ages seemed to range from the late sixties to the late eighties. The leader was a retired University of Missouri journalism professor. Each member wrote and read one of their writings each week. They could write about anything they desired. One woman read a page of a short story she was creating, another read a summary of her recent trip to Brazil. One of the men wrote clever, couplet poetry. Some chose to write original pieces, while one or two often summarized articles written by others. There was no critiquing. The leader was encouraging, but not overly complimentary to any one person. Marvela thought the writing talent ranged from mediocre to quite brilliant. She definitely wanted to be a part of the group.

Marvela was discovering positive things about *Forest Glen*, but she still had misgivings about it being the right place for her. She was glad she only had to give one month's notice should she decide to move someday. For now, she would give the place a chance to grow on her.

She went to bed early that night, after making a list of things she needed to accomplish the next day. It was imperative that she find a doctor as soon as possible. She decided to ask her neighbor Ruth for recommendations. Ruth usually had breakfast the same time as Marvela. As it turned out, Ruth's son was an internal medicine physician who accepted Medicare patients. Florence, who was sitting at the same table, related that Dr. Peterson was her physician, and she highly recommended him. Marvela asked the women to suggest an ophthalmologist as well. She spent most of the day making doctor's appointments.

At dinner that night, she chose to sit at a table for two. She was examining the menu when a male voice asked, "May I join you?"

Marvela looked up and saw a smiling man in a wheelchair. He looked younger than most of the men she had seen thus far. His hair was gray and styled a bit like Bill Clinton's. *He's about seventy or possibly younger,* she thought.

"Yes, of course, please have a seat," she smiled as she put down the menu she'd been studying.

His name was Stan Mast. He was a retired Kansas University secondary education professor. He remembered John, but didn't know him well. They had a pleasant conversation, and discovered many things in common.

"Tonight is classics night in our small theater; you might like to attend. *Citizen Kane* is playing," Stan informed her.

"One of my favorites. I haven't seen it in years." Marvela smiled.

"Some of us get together in the pub for a discussion after the movie. The number is dwindling, but we would love to have you join us." Stan's smile lit up his face. He had broad shoulders and looked quite athletic. Marvela wondered why he was in a wheelchair.

As if reading her mind, Stan said, "I've been at *Forest Glen* for almost two years. I was paralyzed in a diving accident and probably won't ever walk—officially a paraplegic. My injury affected the lower spine, so I have a bit more mobility than some paraplegics. I have a great physical therapist that helped me become independent enough to live here. Like Christopher Reeves, I haven't given up all hope, but the advances in research may not come to fruition in my lifetime."

"I've always thought that as long as one can 'hope,' there is HOPE," Marvela smiled, and paused before going on. "I contracted polio when I was eight years old," she continued. "I know it was my mother's clear vision of my ultimate health, and of course her persistent care, that saw me through. Other than a weakness in my left arm, there is no sign of that dreadful disease, so far anyway. Of course my childhood activities were limited for several years. I remember enviously watching other children run and play."

"My childhood wasn't exactly normal," Stan mused, "I was sort of a wimp in elementary school, but had a growth spurt in junior high. Fortunately for me, a coach discovered I had some athletic talent, so I became actively involved in sports throughout high school and college. In fact, I was intensely involved in sports until my accident, which happened during a triathlon competition for seniors."

Marvela wasn't sure how to react. Stan was so matter-of-fact as he told her the circumstances of his injury.

"You have certainly overcome lots of hurdles."

"I was fortunate to be encouraged by some very inspiring people. I'll never forget the words of Mike Shappi, a wheelchair basketball star turned motivational speaker, 'Just because you can't stand up doesn't mean you can't stand out.'"

"In my opinion you're a standout. You look very athletic," Marvela said admiringly.

"Thank you lovely lady, you're quite a standout yourself," Stan quipped.

"There's nothing as uplifting as a mutual admiration society." Marvela laughed. "But seriously, how do you stay so fit?"

"I lift weights daily to keep my upper body strong. I also play some wheelchair basketball. You should come watch some time."

"I'm impressed. Once in New York I saw a wheelchair basketball championship game. It was truly amazing."

Stan laughed, "Our game is very tame, no comparison. Most of us are past middle age, so we do well to make it up and down the court." Marvela smiled, "I'm still impressed."

"Well, it is fun," Stan replied. "You might enjoy watching us. Do you have your own transportation?"

"Not yet. I want to buy a car. I think it would be useful here."

"It would. The bus service here is fairly good, but I'm too impatient to wait around. I drive my own especially equipped van. I can manipulate all driving mechanisms with my hands. It's one of the luxuries I purchased with my insurance money. I'll have to take you for a spin sometime, but now its showtime."

Seven people watched the movie, four stayed for a discussion in the Pub. Stan introduced Jeanne Starr, a former high school French teacher, and Leonard Stinson, a retired pro baseball coach with the Kansas City Royals. He walked with the help of a cane, but Jeanne seemed to get around very well. She had curly, dyed, strawberry blonde hair and sparkling green eyes. Although her face was lined, she had good bone structure and looked years younger than eighty-three. Leonard had a fringe of gray hair and a handlebar mustache. His leathery, wrinkled face showed the effects of years in the sun, but there were more laugh lines than frown lines. The four of them had a lively, involved conversation. Leonard was a movie buff who had seen *Citizen Kane* ten times. He used colorful language, and his loud, infectious laughter punctuated the conversation.

Jeanne whispered to Marvela, "Isn't he a hoot?"

The group conversed for over an hour.

"They roll up the sidewalks around here about eight o'clock, but they keep the place well lit, so the night owls can find their way home." Leonard chuckled.

As they waited for the elevators, Stan told Marvela that Jeanne and Leonard, both eighty-three, would be getting married over the Christmas holidays when their families could attend the ceremony.

"In the meantime, they share an apartment. It's an economical advantage, but I really think that couple is in love," Stan added. Stan boarded the elevator to the first floor and waved good-bye to Marvela who was waiting for the second elevator to take her to the third floor.

She felt a surge of optimism about *Forest Glen*. Meeting Stan was a pleasant surprise. She hoped they would become good friends.

CHAPTER FOUR

When Marvela awoke the following morning, she felt energetic and ready to do most of her exercise routine—a combination of Yoga and stretching. She had recently added some Tibetan exercises that were supposedly designed to prolong youth. She wasn't able to do all of her routine; her left knee was still not flexible enough to do some of the stretches. But she vowed to continue trying, hoping her flexibility would improve in time. After exercising, she spent some time hanging up her clothes. She would need some under the bed storage boxes and some over the door hangers. She dreaded waiting for bus service to the mall to make these purchases. There was no doubt she needed a car. She went to the front desk to check out the bus schedule, and then stopped at the computer room where she logged on to her e-mail website. She was delighted to find an e-mail from Ron. He stated that he wanted to stop by Kansas City that weekend. He was on his way to New York for a meeting, and would like to stay over two nights. She replied immediately.

It will be wonderful to see you, Ron. We have so much catching up to do. Can't wait! Marvela composed an e-mail to Marie, cc'd it to Steve, detailing more of her impressions of *Forest Glen* and telling them about Ron's upcoming visit. She met Ron in the lobby Saturday morning, and stood looking him over after they hugged. He looked so much like John. He had the same tousled look and shy grin.

"You look good, Ron, but I think you've lost weight, you're very thin."
"Yeah, life has been rather hectic lately. There's been little time for eating, or sleep for that matter. Things are heating up with elections coming soon."

"I've stocked up on your favorite snacks, and hopefully you can catch up on some sleep. Other than helping me choose a car, there's nothing on the agenda." Marvela squeezed his arm. "You really don't have to help me do that either."

"I'd love to go car shopping with you, Mom. Do you have a current driver's license?"

"Yes, I keep it renewed, since it's an important ID."

They had a great weekend. Ron helped Marvela select a silver Honda Civic at a special discount price for end-of-the-year models. She'd debated about purchasing a Hybrid, but after discussing the pros and cons with Ron, they decided she wouldn't drive it enough to make up the extra ticket price.

"Why don't you take your new car for a spin?" Ron suggested. "It's been a long time since you've driven."

"You're right. I doubt if I have been behind the wheel more than a half dozen times in the last thirty years."

"I remember you rented a car a number of times to take us to Aunt Sylvia's."

"We had some good times, didn't we, Ron?"

"For the most part I have good memories, except for some of the awful schools." Ron made a face.

"The decision to place you boys in a private school, after your bad public school experiences, was probably one of the best I've ever made. Of course I couldn't have swung it without some help from Sylvia."

"Good old Aunt Sylvia. She was always there for us, wasn't she?"

"I don't know how I would have gotten along without her, especially after the divorce." Marvela said with conviction.

"I remember well the good times we had at her house on the beach. I learned to swim and sail there. Sylvia was a kind of Aunt Mame, wasn't she?"

"She didn't take on those characteristics until she quit her moderately salaried publishing job, and married her rich boss," Marvela reminded him.

"I remember Phil. They would bring us souvenirs from their many travels. Didn't he die of Parkinson's?"

"Yes, Sylvia was his caretaker the last years of his life. She was a grand lady, supportive and generous until the end. Although Phil left the bulk of his estate to her, his children ended up with his money after Sylvia died. She thought she had left me a sizable inheritance, but that wasn't meant to be."

"You've done OK without it, Mom." Ron squeezed her hand.

"For sure. I wasn't about to get caught up in a court battle with Phil's children."

Marvela patted her new purchase. "I like it, let's go."

"Don't forget to adjust the mirrors, Mom." Ron cautioned.

Marvela loved the feel of the new car, and soon felt comfortable driving.

"Like riding a bicycle, you don't forget. My dad taught me to drive when I was twelve years old. Of course, we only drove on country roads. Dad was so patient with me." Marvela felt a surge of nostalgia.

"Have you ever been back to Hubbardsville?"

"Only once. The Nobles had a family reunion about fifteen years ago. The aunts and uncles were deceased, and I met cousins I didn't know I had, but other than sending occasional Christmas cards, I haven't kept up with them."

"I remember you telling us they were a real conservative bunch."

"Right, there wasn't much we had in common. After one disastrous argument, I kept my mouth shut. Dad was a maverick in that group. I still miss the conversations we had. He was open-minded about most things." Tears formed in Marvela's eyes.

"Are you lonely, Mom?" Ron asked, putting his hand on hers.

"I wouldn't be honest if I said I wasn't, but I'm grateful for my ability to make friends, and I expect to make at least a few good ones at *Forest Glen*."

"I'll try to stop by whenever I travel to the east coast," Ron promised. The time with Ron flew by. Marvela hated to see him leave, but was grateful he had taken the time to make the extra stop. She worried about Ron. He was devoted to his work, but she knew he was still looking for the right companion. After six months of marriage, his first wife left him for a woman. Ten years later, the memory still haunted him. Marvela tried not to shed tears as she kissed Ron good-bye. "Remember to push the reply button on your e-mail. Just tell me you're OK."

When Marvela went to the dining room that evening she looked around for Stan, but didn't see him. Jeanne and Leonard motioned for her to join them. As usual the conversation was lively. Leonard's loud laughter caused several of the diners to look at him disapprovingly.

Jeanne waved at them and smiled. "Laughter is the best medicine, you know," she said as she patted Leonard's arm.

Marvela asked if they had seen Stan lately.

"He's in the hospital for his semiannual tests," Leonard replied.

"He doesn't want to miss any cutting-edge research," Jeanne added. He has signed up for experimental treatments at NIH, and may have to spend some time in Washington."

"If determination and perseverance would make the difference, Stan would be walking now," Leonard commented.

Marvela decided to go for a walk after dinner. The evening was fairly cool for late August. She walked to a well-kept flower garden on the *Forest Glen* campus. She was amazed at the variety of flowers and the artful design of the place. She found a glider across from a small waterfall that emptied into fishpond, and sat watching the goldfish. It was a quiet, peaceful setting, and she soon nodded off. In a dream, John came to sit beside her, and told her of his desire to live in a place where he could have a fishpond. When she shook herself awake, she remembered how real John's presence felt in the dream. She wondered if John had ever built a koi pond, one of his fantasies when they lived in New York City. The chirping of a flock of birds landing in grove of trees caught her attention. One blackbird landed on the glider, close enough to touch. It cocked its head and looked up at her, as though it wanted to speak before flying off. Marvela laughed and said out loud, "John, you old devil!"

Before leaving, she walked to a grove of trees and listened to the rustle of the leaves and the chirping of birds. She let her imagination soar, and imagined a host of angels calling out to her. She felt calm and peaceful under the trees. *Forest Glen* was certainly an appropriate name for the place. She vowed to return to the idyllic spot, and resume the meditation practice she had neglected for many months.

The following morning on her way to breakfast, she caught up with a woman taking slow, halting steps behind a walker. Since many of the residents were sensitive about accepting help, she hesitated, until the woman nearly fell.

"Is there something I can do to help you?" Marvela offered. She introduced herself. "I'm Marvela Higglesford; I believe I'm your neighbor across the hall."

"Pleased to—meet you—Marvela. My name is . . . Flora Pattenella," she responded laboriously. "I wish . . . I could tell you . . . I didn't need help, but . . . that is . . . not the case." She stopped often for breath, and nearly fell again. Marvela took hold of her arm.

"Would you like to go back to your apartment? I'll be glad to call the nurse for you." Flora seemed to get a second wind, "Please help me to my apartment, but don't call the nurse." At the apartment, Flora asked Marvela to help her into her recliner. "I spend most days and nights here," Flora informed her. "My oxygen machine is over there." She pointed. "Would you . . . mind helping me . . . get hooked up?" She asked breathlessly. Marvela brought the machine over, and Flora told her how to hook it up. After a few deep breaths she confided, "I thought I could do without this appendage while I went to get something to eat, but I was wrong. I haven't had anything to eat since day before yesterday, and food is worth my taking a risk."

"Couldn't you have called for meal service?" Marvela asked.

"I could have, but chose not to," Flora replied with a sigh. She took a few more deep breaths of oxygen. Marvela waited for her to continue.

"They have threatened to send me to assisted living. I probably belong there, but I'm ninety years old, and have nearly used up my savings. I could possibly get Medicaid, or some such help, but I'm a proud old crone." She grinned at Marvela. "They lock you in over there, and I hate that. My mind is still good, and so many of the residents in assisted living seem out of it. I was there for six months after a light stroke kept me from walking for a while, and didn't like it one bit. When I was able to walk with assistance," she pointed to the walker, "they gave in to my insistence, and let me move back to Independent Living, but I'm walking a thin line." She started to cough.

Marvela handed her a tissue.

Flora straightened her shoulders and made an effort to talk normally. "If you would get me some milk and a roll from the breakfast bar, I would be ever so grateful."

Marvela brought her the food she requested, and added a banana and apple.

"Thank you, you're a dear. I think that's all I need now." Flora forced a smile and nodded to the door.

Marvela had mixed feeling about leaving her alone. "Flora, I'm going to leave my phone number by your telephone. Please call me if you need anything. If you promise that, I won't call the nurse." Marvela feared she sounded too threatening.

But Flora nodded in agreement. "I will call you, and thanks again for your help."

Back in her apartment, Marvela wondered if she had done the right thing. Even if Flora didn't call, she would look in on her at mealtimes, and make sure she had food. She shared her concerns with Ruth, who didn't want to get involved.

"Flora is one of several who should be in assisted living. I don't want to encourage them to try to make it on their own," Ruth said dismissively.

Marvela decided to be supportive of Flora for a while longer. She brought meals to Flora for the next five days. Fortunately, the hostess at the dining room didn't question her about asking for so many meals in boxes.

For the first few days Flora picked at her food, but about the third day her appetite started to improve, and she seemed to gain some energy. She had a delightful sense of humor, and Marvela enjoyed her company. Flora had been a physical therapist, and had worked until she was sixty-eight. She and her second husband enjoyed their retirement and traveled extensively, until he died of a heart attack ten years ago. For the next five years, Flora lived alone in a comfortable home, and hired landscape people to keep up her large yard. She continued to travel until she began to have trouble walking without help due to encroaching arthritis. Flora chose to live at *Forest Glen*, because they allowed people who needed walkers and wheelchairs to be housed in Independent Living.

Flora had thick gray hair, cut quite stylishly. Her face was lined, but still quite lovely, especially when she smiled.

"I really like your hairstyle. You have evidently visited the beauty shop here," Marvela said admiringly.

"Yes, the beauticians are really quite good. They probably do more to keep up our morale than anyone else around here," Flora said nodding her head.

"Do you set up regular weekly appointments?

"I can't always make it, but was able to get there last week, thank goodness," she sighed. "My daughter, Marian, from Los Angeles is flying in to visit me this weekend, and of course I want to look my best."

That evening when Marvela brought her dinner she said emphatically, "It's imperative that I walk to the dining room to eat with Marian. She'll definitely recommend assisted living if she thinks I can't get there on my own."

"Would you like to practice walking today?" Marvela inquired. "I'll be glad to walk with you."

"That's a good idea. Thank you for the offer. Getting out of this chair will probably be the most difficult part."

Marvela helped the frail woman stand, and brought her walker to her. "Do you want me to carry your oxygen tank?"

"I'll inhale a few deep breaths, and see if I can do without it."

Flora took labored steps down the hall and back. When they arrived back at her apartment, she was gasping for breath.

"It might be a good idea to take your oxygen tank with you when you walk," Marvela suggested gently as she helped Flora into her chair and hooked up the tank.

Flora nodded. "Marian knows I need the oxygen, so she will insist that I take it with me to the dining room."

"What would we do without daughters to 'mother' us." Marvela chuckled.

Flora paused, frowning a bit before she spoke. "I guess I wouldn't mind a little more of the 'mothering' you speak of." She laughed somewhat caustically. "But maybe it's for the best."

Marvela wasn't sure how to respond. "I guess mother-daughter relationships can get a bit touchy at times," she ventured.

Flora nodded. "I don't think you meant touchy-feely, did you?" She grinned at Marvela.

Marvela wondered about Flora's relationship to her daughter, but decided not to pursue the topic.

The next morning at breakfast, Marvela saw Flora enter with Marian. Flora wore makeup and a freshly ironed yellow linen pantsuit. She looked happy and seemed quite energetic. After Marvela finished eating, she stopped at their table and got acquainted with Flora's daughter. Marian was impeccably groomed; her highlighted short brown hair was styled becomingly. Marvela guessed her to be in the late fifties, although she could be older.

"Mother loves having you as a neighbor. She says you take walks together." Marian shook Marvela's hand and Flora winked at her.

"How long are you staying, Marian?" Marvela inquired.

"Unfortunately I have to go back tomorrow. I am involved in a controversial court case. We go to trial next week."

"Marian is a busy trial lawyer," Flora explained. "Her visits are always short, but sweet." She patted Marian's arm. Marvela thought she saw Marian frown.

"I would feel better if mother was in assisted living." Marian shook her head and looked despairingly at her mother, "But she is determined to be independent. Although she does seem to be doing OK, don't you think?"

Marvela hesitated before speaking, "She certainly looks perky today. You can rest assured that I will check on her to make sure she is all right."

Flora breathed a visible sigh of relief. "Marvela is wonderful company." She gave Marvela a conspiratorial look.

After Marian went back to Los Angeles, Flora seemed revived. She got along quite well for several weeks, and was able to go to the dining room with Marvela's help. But one day, she told Marvela she didn't think she could make it to the dining room, so Marvela went back to bringing her meals. The dining room hostess was evidently used to getting meals in boxes for some of the residents, for she didn't complain. Marvela always checked on Flora before she went to bed. Since Flora chose to sleep in her recliner, Marvela tried to make her as comfortable as possible by bringing extra pillows and blankets.

"Marvela, I really appreciate your 'mothering.' You could spoil me, you know."

"Flora, I like doing things for you. My mother died in her prime, so I didn't get to do for her. I hope you don't mind being a sort of surrogate." Marvela hugged her. "And of course a good friend."

"Having you around to help me is one of the best things that has happened to me recently. If in some way I can be a stand-in for the mother you didn't see age, I consider it a joy and privilege." She reached over to kiss Marvela's cheek.

CHAPTER FIVE

Marvela enjoyed her visits with Flora. She had such a lively sense of humor, and despite her handicaps, she was an amazingly positive person.

One morning when Marvela brought Flora's breakfast, she noticed with alarm that the oxygen tubes were not in place. Flora's head was on her chest and her eyes were closed. Marvela felt her wrist and detected a faint pulse. She pressed the button on the lifeline Flora wore around her neck, and tried to get the oxygen tubes back in her nose. Nothing seemed to be coming through. She shook the tank and determined it was empty.

In about four minutes the nurse rushed in. He took Flora's pulse and immediately called for help on his cell phone. Marvela watched as Flora was placed on a stretcher, an easy task since she was so light, mainly skin and bones. Her lips were turning blue and she seemed to be in a deep coma. At the health care center, she was given emergency treatment. Her eyes fluttered, and some color returned to her face after she received oxygen and a shot of glucose. The nurse attached IV tubes and hooked Florence to a heart monitor.

Marvela looked on as the nurses worked over the frail body.

"The doctor should be here momentarily," one of the nurses told Marvela. "Are you related to her?" Marvel shook her head. "We need to notify her next of kin immediately. She may not recover," the nurse said wearily.

She had Marian's phone number, so Marvela took out the address book she carried in her purse, pulled out her cell phone, and punched in the numbers.

After several rings, Marian answered. Marvela told her about Flora's condition.

"It will be at least a day or two before I can get away. There are so many pressing things I must tend to here. I am on my way to the courthouse now. I will try to get the trial postponed, but it won't be easy," Marian said with a tinge of impatience.

"Are there any other relatives that should be notified?" Marvela asked, astounded at Marian's cold response.

"Not really, I'm an only child, as you know, and I've never married. There may be some cousins, but I have lost track of them."

"Marian, please come as soon as possible," Marvel said with urgency. "Your mother may not make it."

Marian's tone softened. "I'll get there as soon as I possibly can. Thank you for being there."

Marvela's hands shook as she put away her cell phone. Back in her apartment, she thought about other residents in the retirement community, and wondered *how many had children like Marian, or maybe none at all.* She felt a need to talk to Marie.

Marie answered on the first ring. "Is everything OK, Mom?"

"I'm fine, just needed to hear your voice," Marvela told Marie about the turn Flora had taken.

"Oh, Mom, what a shame. Flora sounded like such a neat person. You can be assured that if anything happened to you, I would be on the first flight I could get," Marie said with emotion.

"Not a day passes that I don't give thanks for a daughter like you." They talked for about an hour. Marvela felt better when she hung up. She took a quick shower, found some clothes that weren't too wrinkled, ran a comb through her hair, refreshed her lipstick, and made her way back to Flora's room. She got there just as a nurse and a doctor rushed into the room.

"It's a code blue!" the nurse exclaimed breathlessly. "If you're related, you may come in."

Marvela entered without hesitating. She stood in the back of the room and watched the medics work on Flora. When she eyed the heart monitor, there didn't seem to be any movement.

"She's gone," the doctor said as he placed the chest clappers on the bedside table.

The nurse looked at Marvela. "Are you the daughter?"

"No, but I seem to be her only friend," Marvela replied. "I'll call her daughter, Marian, in Los Angeles," Marvela said with a sigh. "She'll need to make the burial arrangements."

"Use the phone at the nurse's station. We'll take care of the body. Would you like to spend some time with uh," the nurse looked at the chart, "Flora?"

Marvela nodded, walked to the bed, and took Flora's hand. She offered a silent prayer and murmured, "Good-bye, dear friend, may you rest in peace." It took several tries before Marvela was able to speak to Marian, who had to be called out of the courtroom.

"Marian, I have some bad news, your mother died just a few minutes ago. I assume you will be here as soon as possible."

There was a pause. "Marvela, I know this sounds awful, but I can't get away now. I was unable to postpone the trial, and it would be next to impossible for me to leave at this time."

Marvela stammered, "M—Marian, this is unbelievable."

"But true, unfortunately," Marian responded with a slight catch in her voice. "Everything is in order. I helped mother make advance burial arrangements. She wants—wanted—to be cremated. I'll call the funeral home," Marian took a deep breath. "I'm sorry things had to turn out this way."

"What about her things? I would guess that her apartment will need to be cleared soon," Marvela asked, trying to keep her voice calm.

"I'll call a moving company. They can take the furniture and clothes to a charitable organization. There's really nothing there that I want. If you find something you would like to have, help yourself." She paused. "I need to get back now. Call me tonight if you have questions. Again, thank you for being there." Her voice was without emotion.

Marvela hung up the phone and stared into space, unwilling to believe what she had just heard. "She's not coming."

The nurse at the desk looked at her questioningly. Marvela summarized the situation.

"That is really not too unusual for a number of residents here. Out of sight, out of mind." The nurse shook her head.

When Marvela got back to Flora's room, the body was being placed on a gurney. Marvela watched as the attendants took Flora down the hall. There was no more she could do for her. After dinner that evening, Marvela called Marian, making sure it was after nine Pacific time.

"I'm sure you think I'm cold and uncaring," Marian commented, "but mother and I have never been close. I have tried to make sure she was well cared for."

Marvela couldn't help but respond, "It's such a contrast to the relationship I have with my three children."

Marian cleared her throat, "I was close to my father. He died in a hunting accident soon after I graduated from law school." She continued hoarsely near tears, "I guess I never really got over his death. Mother married again less than a year later. I never quite forgave her for finding someone else so soon." Her tone changed to her usual briskness. "Enough of that. Is there something more I need to do?"

"Do you have any plans for a memorial service?"

"Not really, I'm sure there is someone at *Forest Glen* who will arrange something in-house."

"I will check with the activities director. We'll try to come up with something appropriate," Marvela said, trying to keep her voice level.

"Would you order a nice bouquet of flowers and have it billed to me?" Marian asked in a gentler tone of voice.

"I'll do that, and I'll keep you posted on the arrangements we'll make. I haven't been here long, so I'll need to check around."

"I trust that you will do the right thing, Marvela. I do appreciate your involvement," she said rather unconvincingly.

Marvela felt a surge of anger toward Marian as she hung up the phone, but she was determined to make sure Flora was remembered with dignity. She crossed the hall to Flora's apartment. The door was unlocked, so she entered, and looked around. As she ran her hands over the recliner where Flora spent so much time, she had a feeling that Flora was in the room with her.

"It's OK, Flora. No more suffering." Marvela wiped a tear. "We didn't know each other long, but I loved you." She decided to call the administrative offices and the activities director before she did anything more.

The head administrator wasn't in, but his secretary said she'd inform him of the situation. Kyle, the activities director, told her he would be right up to help make decisions. He asked Marvela to relate all of the details. She found him sympathetic and helpful. Kyle informed her that a resident, Jane Watson, had recently been appointed to help arrange events like memorial services, and offered to set up a meeting with her.

They met the next morning and made arrangements for a memorial service on Sunday afternoon—three days away. Kyle suggested the service be held in the atrium. Piano music could be provided by Ahna, a resident who played beautifully. Jane thought they should set up a table with pictures of Flora, and possibly a few memorabilia. Marvela informed them that Flora's daughter could not be present, but would send flowers.

Jane grimaced, and shook her head. "I met Marian once. I wasn't impressed."

Marvela was grateful for Jane's help. Jane, a spry eighty-year-old with beautifully coiffed white hair, had a quick smile, and laughed easily. Jane offered to help Marvela find appropriate pictures among Flora's things. They went through a number of drawers before they found some pictures of Flora. One, a graduation picture, was a photo of a beautiful long-haired blonde smiling impishly at the camera. A wedding picture portrayed Flora in a white satin gown, being kissed by a darkly handsome groom, holding up her short veil. There were several pictures of Flora with Marian as a baby and toddler. In a drawer by a table near her recliner, they found a picture of an older, but still lovely, Flora with a graying middle-aged man. There was also a packet of letters in that drawer.

Marvela explained to Jane, "Flora's daughter told me her mother married again shortly after her first husband died. This must be the second husband's picture, and the letters are probably from him."

"I didn't know Flora very well," Jane mused. "She played bridge with us a few times, but seemed to lose interest . . . definitely a loner. Unfortunately there are too many people like her in this place. If the residents don't make the effort, there really are few attempts to get them involved in social activities."

"I only knew Flora about three months, but I felt we were good friends," Marvela commented. "I was surprised there weren't more efforts to check on her. Of course she feared being sent to assisted living."

"That too is typical. The fees are very high there, and people do value their independence," Jane added.

When Jane left, Marvela continued looking for clues to Flora's life. She noted that Flora collected ceramic cats. Marvela decided to pick a few to place on the memorial table. She found about four hundred dollars in a kitchen drawer. That would buy more flowers, and maybe something else for the memorial service. The checkbook and other financial papers she would send to Marian, as well as some jewelry which looked valuable. She would keep some of the costume pieces, as Marian had suggested. She took the packet of letters with her when she left. While she hated to impose on privacy, the letters might offer some clues that would be helpful in preparing some kind of obituary.

At bedtime, she turned on her reading light and opened the packet of letters. She held them in her hand for a moment before opening the first one. "Forgive me, Flora." They read like a soap opera. It seems Flora and Ray, a physician, had an affair before the death of Flora's first husband. Ray was also married. They worked at the same hospital, and have exchanged confidences about their miserable marriages before they became lovers. Flora's husband Dwight cheated on her constantly, and Ray's wife was a spoiled debutante who refused to have sex after their honeymoon.

Marvela wondered if Marian knew about Dwight's philandering. Probably not, for according to the letters, Flora wanted to keep Marian sheltered from the truth. Flora and Ray were deeply in love, and they seemed to enjoy a happy marriage. The letters referred to the rift between Flora and Marian, something Flora tried hard to overcome.

Marvela checked her watch and decided that midnight central time wasn't too late to call Marian in California. The phone rang at least ten times before Marian picked it up.

"I hope I didn't wake you, but I wanted to tell you about the plans for the memorial service," Marvela said tactfully.

"Marian's voice was slurred, "I was asleep, but go ahead." Marvela related the plans, and told her about the cash she had found, and her desire to spend it on the memorial service.

"I'm sure I can trust your judgment, Marvela," Marian commented dryly. Marvela hesitated before asking, "Marian, do you think any of Ray's people would like to come to the service?"

"Absolutely not," Marian responded indignantly, "besides, I have no idea how to get in touch with them." Her voice softened a bit. "Thank you for sharing the memorial plans, please do what you think best about spending the money you found." She yawned. "I need to get some sleep; tomorrow will be a trying day."

"I hope you sleep well, Marian." Marvela couldn't keep the edge out of her voice. She hung up the phone and made some notes about the memorial service. One of the letters referred to a brother of Ray's who lived in Kansas City. Marvela decided to try and get in touch with him. She was beyond sleep, so she got the telephone book and looked up Donald Pattenella. There were only two listed. She would try both numbers in the morning.

As Marvela thought about the memorial service, it occurred to her that she would like to spend some of Flora's money on memorial bookmarks to hand out at the service. She could use Flora's graduation picture, as well as a more recent one she had found, along with the obituary she would write.

In the morning Marvela called both Pattenellas, and discovered they were father and son. They were pleased to hear from her, and both agreed to attend Flora's memorial service with their families. The elder would come with his wife, and the younger would attend with his wife and two teenage children.

About forty residents showed up for the service. Ahna played for about fifteen minutes until all were seated. Marvela asked Don senior to say a few words about his memories of Flora. He spoke eloquently about the happy marriage between his brother and Flora, and shared some stories relating how Flora had helped many people. Marvela read the obituary, which she had pieced together from letters, her conversations with Flora, and events Don was able to share. One of the residents played a violin number, and Ahna continued playing soft music, while Marvela and Jane handed out the bookmarks.

Marvela taped the proceedings to send Marian, along with the extra bookmarks. She hoped Marian would be able to find addresses of some relatives who might appreciate the sentiment.

When Marvela checked her mail the next day, she found a formal letter from the CEO of *Forest Glen*, thanking her for her help in arranging the memorial service. A week later, she received a letter from Marian. In it she apologized for her lack of support during her mother's illness and death.

"I was so preoccupied with the trial, I probably wasn't thinking clearly." Marian wrote. She thanked Marvela for all she had done, and added a special thanks for Marvela's thoughtfulness in sending the bookmarks and the taped proceedings of the memorial service.

Too little too late, Marvela thought.

CHAPTER SIX

Marvela did little but read and sleep for three days after Flora's memorial service. She soon began to feel bored, so she was delighted to receive an e-mail from her son, Steve, inviting her to join him and his family for a long weekend at Branson, Missouri. The thought of seeing her grandchildren meant more to her than the shows, so she offered to babysit while Steve and his wife Sonia attended a number of events. Marvela and the children enjoyed boat rides on the lake, and had a great time touring Silver Dollar City.

The children were patient with her slow pace, and asked her if they could decorate her cane. They bought balloons and fastened one on Marvela's wooden cane. She loved being a grandmother, and regretted the fact that she didn't get to see more of her grandchildren—three-year-old Susan, and five-year-old Andrew. She took lots of pictures to share with Marie and Ron. Steve and Sonia were grateful for the babysitting, and Marvela was pleased with the opportunity to get better acquainted with Sonia. She had been quite fond of Steve's first wife, and still kept in touch with her. The coolness between Sonia and her mother-in-law warmed up considerably during this visit. Marvela felt encouraged.

When she returned to *Forest Glen*, she made a point to speak with Kyle about doing some volunteering. He was delighted, and asked her if she would like to call bingo at one of the assisted living centers. She agreed to call every Thursday evening after dinner for eight to ten regular bingo players. Kyle warned her that Alice, one of the players, would try to take over the proceedings. So Marvela tactfully told the group she would do her best to be fair, but Kyle had given her the authority to make decisions. She noticed that Alice, a wizened little woman with a piercing voice, brought the same three bingo cards with her every session. The others felt they could only manage one or two, which they selected from the stack each week. It was obvious they resented Alice, who had an unfair advantage, and won most of the games. Marvela decided she would try to address the injustice. One night she asked the group to vote on whether there should be a rule that no more than two cards be played, and they should be selected from the stack. All but Alice voted in favor of this arrangement. The next day Kyle told Marvela that Alice complained to him that Marvela "picked on her." She laughed and told Kyle about the vote.

"I think the other seven really felt empowered by the outcome, and Alice didn't win most of the games anymore," Marvela said, feeling she had found a solution to the unfair situation.

To her surprise, Kyle told her that it might be best to let Alice continue playing with her three cards.

Marvela told him it had become a matter of principle with her. "Maybe, I shouldn't continue to call bingo."

"I understood your feelings, Marvela, but I do hope you will reconsider." Kyle pulled on his chin. "That Alice can cause a lot of trouble."

Marvela told Marie about the situation in their next phone conversation.

Marie laughed. "Mother, remember how your 'principles' almost got you fired from ABC?"

"All too well," Marvela said with a shudder. "A valued colleague was laid off when she reached sixty-five. Nina was an excellent writer and had glowing evaluations. She was in good health, and wanted to keep working. It was a clear case of age discrimination, so I went straight to the top and complained about the injustice."

Marie added, "And you were told to keep your opinions out of any decisions regarding personnel or else . . ."

"It was tough, but I didn't want to lose my job, so I apologized for speaking my mind. Volunteering for bingo is quite dispensable, and since it's such a trifling matter, I guess I'll keep calling and allow that spitfire Alice to play her three cards. I probably owe it to the other ladies. Essie, a stroke victim, said the other night in her wavering voice, 'I love you.'"

"And I love you. You'll always be my hero, Mom."

Marvela breathed a prayer of thanksgiving as she hung up, thinking of Marian and Flora.

That night at dinner, Stan beckoned her to sit with him. She hadn't spoken to him at any length for over a month. They had a pleasant conversation. He told her that he was in an experimental program at the National Institute for Health, which required that he travel to Washington twice a month for treatments.

"My goal is to gain enough strength and flexibility in my legs to be able to walk with braces. I have a standing apparatus which helps with circulation."

"I have a feeling you will realize that dream," Marvela said as she put her hand on his. He put his other hand on hers.

"Thanks for the vote of confidence. By the way, would you like to take a drive with me tomorrow?" Stan asked. "I need to go to the mall on Ninety-fifth Street, and I thought you might want to do some shopping there."

"I'd love to go. And yes, I would like to do some shopping. I haven't bought any new clothes for ages." Marvela smiled, delighted to have the opportunity to spend more time with Stan.

They had a great time. After sharing a latte at Starbucks, they went their separate ways, planning to meet at Starbucks in two hours. Both liked lattes, and thought they should indulge their tastes. Marvela bought two pairs of slacks and three new tops, suitable for the casual dress at *Forest Glen*. She hadn't seen any of the women in jeans, so she had packed hers away in favor of slacks and some bright tops.

Back at her apartment, she checked her answering machine—there was one message.

"Hi Marvela, surprise! I wonder if you'll recognize my voice."

It was John! He still had an unmistakable deep bass voice.

"Marie gave me your number, so I decided to call you. I can't believe you left New York City." He gave his number. "Call me back when it suits you."

Marvela sank into the sofa in shock. She hadn't heard his voice in fourteen years. She had to admit, it still gave her a small thrill. She had always loved his voice.

She dialed Marie's number. "Why did you do it, Marie?"

"Oh, hi, Mom. Do what?" she replied innocently.

"You know what I'm talking about."

"Yeah, Mom. I'll have to admit I've never given up on you guys getting together."

"Well, it's a little late for that," Marvela said with a tinge of regret.

"Actually, when I told Dad where you were living, he asked for your number," Marie explained.

"I'm not sure I'll call him back. No use in waking up sleeping dogs." Marvela laughed.

"Try it, you might like it." Marie giggled. "You've always wanted a dog."

"Marie Higglesford, I should spank you!"

"Remember the last time you tried," Marie challenged.

"I do. After one hard slap on your bottom, you yelled to high heaven, and I sat down and cried with you. It was the last and only time I resorted to hitting my children."

"You told me later that one of your favorite psychology teachers said, 'People aren't for hitting,'" Marie remembered. "If I ever have children that will be my motto as well. Excuse me, Mom. I think Nigel is trying to call me. We'll talk more later."

"Tell that lucky man, hi," After Marvela hung up she allowed herself to reminisce. She had to admit the boys were a handful at times. She remembered when five-year-old Steve ran into the street after a ball and almost got run over by a truck. She could still hear the squealing of the brakes. Her first impulse was to swat him as hard as she dared, until she saw his terror-stricken face. So she set him on a chair and held his arms tightly.

"Steve, what have I told you about crossing the street?" she asked sternly.

He wiped his tears with his sleeve and sniffled. "Y—you said I should never run out into the streets."

"And what else?" He tried to wiggle out of her grasp, but she held on firmly.

"I should look both ways before crossing the street."

Three-year-old Ron was taking it all in, wide-eyed. Marvela looked at him.

"What could happen if you run into the street without looking, Ron?"

"You'd get hit by a big truck," Ron answered promptly as he spread his arms.

At this Steve burst into tears.

"Steve, what should I do to help you remember?"

"P-pray for me."

Marvela held in her laughter at that response. She hugged both boys, "I always remember you in my prayers, but it's up to you to think before you cross the street." Marvela smiled as she remembered her towheaded boys. Marie was dark-haired and brown-eyed like her father. The boys would vacillate between indulging their little sister and tormenting her. Marie wanted to be included in all of their activities. When they ran from her, she would come to Marvela and plead, "Hold me, those naughty boys won't play with me." Marvela would usually stop whatever she was doing and comfort her daughter. She held and rocked her long after she was a baby. Fortunately such indulgences didn't seem to spoil the little imp.

Interesting how Marie had managed to stay close to both of her parents. Marvela thought guiltily about how John had missed so much of the children's childhood. Maybe she should call him back. They did have the children in common. She looked up his number and dialed, almost hanging up before he answered.

"Hello, this is John Higglesford." His voice hadn't changed.

Marvela paused for a moment. "Hi, this is Marvela."

"There could only be one Marvela. Thanks for returning my call. I got your number from Marie, you know."

"Yes, I know. How are you?"

He told her about his recovery from knee replacement surgery, and she told him about breaking her kneecap.

"I still have to use a cane, how about you?" John inquired. They shared knee therapy experiences, but soon found themselves at loss for further topics to discuss.

Finally, John inquired, "Are you planning to go to Marie's wedding?"

"Definitely," Marvela replied without hesitation.

After another pause, John asked tentatively, "Do you think we might plan on going together?"

"It's a possibility," Marvela replied, and then added impulsively, "I've been looking at old photo albums of the children. Would you like to see them?"

"That would be great, thanks for asking," John replied enthusiastically. They made plans for John to come to Marvela's apartment the following Sunday afternoon. After she hung up, Marvela had second thoughts. She had mixed feelings about seeing John again. There was a lingering bitterness from the custody battles. She was ready to forgive and forget, but wondered about him.

As it turned out, they had a good time looking at the children's pictures. Marvela was pleased she had taken so many. Midway through the journey through time, John paused and turned to Marvela.

"I can't deny that I bore some hostile feelings toward you for taking the children from me, but I will have to admit you did a good job raising them."

Marvela felt her eyes getting moist as she reminded John he did have summers with the children.

John nodded, and added regretfully, "But I couldn't hold on to the boys. They never took to Elaine, who thought I was spoiling them. Also, I felt they faulted me for our breakup."

Marvela told John she had clarified her role in the breakup, but admitted the boys probably held a grudge toward him.

Marvela felt a surge of sympathy toward John. "I have invited the whole family for Thanksgiving. Marie can't make it, but Ron and Steve and his family plan to come. Would you like to join us?"

"I can't think of anything I'd like more." He grasped Marvela's hand. "Thank you, Marvela. I have a deep longing to see my grandchildren."

Marvela booked a private dining room at *Forest Glen* for the family reunion. Ron was pleased his father would be there, but Steve had some misgivings. When Marvela told Steve about Elaine's death he relented.

"He does deserve to see his grandchildren," Steve admitted. "I'll try to prepare Sonia and the children for the encounter," then added, "You aren't planning to go back to him are you, Mom?"

Marvela laughed. "No, dear, but I do have some empathy for his loneliness, and his desire to see his grandchildren."

John arrived early on Thanksgiving Day with a huge bouquet of flowers. Marvela thanked him and found a vase for the flowers. The arrangement featured some huge sunflowers.

"You remembered how I love sunflowers."

"That would be hard to forget. You indulged in fresh sunflowers every time we passed a flower shop." John winked at her. They spent a few minutes recalling other Thanksgiving dinners.

"I remember when Steve broke some plates from your mother's favorite china. You managed to look quite calm, but I could tell you were seething inside," John commented.

"I had to remind myself that Steve was trying to be helpful. I really shouldn't have asked a five-year-old to set the table," Marvela confessed. "As I recall, you were busy carving the turkey and Marie was demanding my attention."

"Those days were hectic, but also quite wonderful." John reached over and kissed Marvela on the cheek.

Just then Ron came into the kitchen, "Am I interrupting something?" John went over to hug him. "We were reminiscing about the good old days." The doorbell rang and Marvela ushered in Steve and his family. Steve shook hands with his father, and introduced his wife and children. Both children went up to their grandfather and kissed him on the cheek.

Steve coached them well, Marvela thought. The day went well. There was a stiff formality between John and Steve, but the children were quite taken with their grandfather, who showed them some of his old magic tricks.

"I remember how I begged you to tell me how you did that." Ron laughed, "But you always told me 'It's magic.'"

John winked at the children. "It is magic, but I might teach you the tricks when you're older."

Steve thought, *he promised me the same thing, but I never learned the secrets.*

Marvela caught Steve's skeptical look and thought, *I need to remind him again that John wanted to keep the family together.*

CHAPTER SEVEN

After Thanksgiving Marvela was swamped with activities and deadlines. Kyle asked her to create a bimonthly newsletter for the residents of *Forest Glen*.

"I like the idea, Kyle. It would definitely help foster a sense of community that is really needed here. But it would be a lot of work. I might consider doing it if I would get some remuneration, like maybe some help with the rent. I can only volunteer for so much," Marvela responded regretfully.

"That's only fair," Kyle replied. "We want you to develop the newsletter for you have the skills we need. I'll check with the CEO and get back to you."

The next day Kyle informed her that Gerald, the CEO, agreed to take a thousand dollars off of her rent if she would do the newsletter twice a month as well as continue her current volunteering. Since this would cut her rent by almost one fourth, Marvela agreed to the terms. She immediately began to brainstorm ideas, scribbling on her trusty yellow pad. She would use bright colors and illustrations. The content would include articles featuring various residents; birthdays would be highlighted. Since so many of the activities Kyle arranged were not well—attended, there could be a section in which residents would give feedback about events they attended, and offer suggestions for activities that would be more interesting to them. A man-on-the-street format could be used for on-the-spot interviews. She soon had pages of ideas.

She showed them to Kyle, and to Stan, Jeanne, and Leonard. They voiced their unanimous approval. Leonard suggested adding jokes. Stan knew a former comic strip artist who lived at *Forest Glen*.

"He might develop an original comic strip for the newsletter. I'd like to see him use his talents. He's in a wheelchair, but there's nothing wrong with his hands—or mind."

Marvela followed up on Stan's suggestion and contacted the artist, Felix O'Connor. He said he would give the idea some thought, and would get back to her. At dinner the following evening she brainstormed with the trio about a name for the newsletter.

"How about *Forest Glen* Leaves?" Jeanne offered.

"Where did he go?" Leonard chuckled. Jeanne slapped his arm.

"I've thought about names related to trees, but couldn't come up with one that worked," Marvela said smiling at Jeanne.

"It's not original, or even clever, but how about *New Horizons?*" Stan mused.

"The logo could be a sun rising over the horizon." He sketched on a napkin.

"It certainly fits the concepts we're trying to promote." Marvela nodded her approval. "Why don't we give it a try? We could ask the residents to submit other titles for future issues."

Since the second newsletter would be close to Christmas, Marvela wanted to put out a special holiday edition. She had asked a number of residents to relate stories of memorable Christmases, so she had a lot of interesting material. Some of them had pictures to illustrate their stories. One resident told of a Christmas when an orange was a treasured gift. Others told of homemade presents, and strings of popcorn and cranberries on a tree they had cut in a nearby forest. One resident told a tragic story of a fire on Christmas eve that destroyed the home. Neighbors took them in and shared their gifts. They said the spirit of Christmas was never more evident.

Marvela worked late every night for a week on that edition, but it was worth it; the residents loved it.

The other outstanding holiday event was Jeanne and Leonard's wedding. Since Marvela's family had been together for Thanksgiving, they chose not to gather again at Christmas. Marie and Steve would spend the holidays with their respective in-laws. Ron planned to spend New Year's Day with his mother. Marvela spent several hours with Jeanne and Jane making wedding plans.

Once again Marvela was planning an event with Jane; this time for a happy occasion. Jane suggested that a string quartet, made up of *Forest Glen* residents, play for the ceremony,

"I like to use the talent we have here. There are several retired symphony orchestra members who play very well," Jane commented. "They walk with difficulty, but they play beautifully," she added.

The atrium was already tastefully decorated for Christmas. The live Christmas tree, featuring white angels and gold bows, reached the second floor of the atrium. Red poinsettias were lined up on either side of the fireplace, and a glittering arrangement of silver and gold ornaments graced the mantel. Marvela suggested the addition of white poinsettias would be perfect for the wedding.

Jeanne wanted a formal ceremony, which pleased Marvela, for she had the perfect gown—a red chiffon with a long flowing skirt. She had worn it only once to a Christmas party for the ABC production staff. What a gala affair it had been! She was escorted by Roger, a handsome producer, one of her circle of gay friends. What memories!

Jeanne had eloped for her first marriage, so this time she decided to wear her mother's white silk wedding gown, which she had kept all of these years. She didn't want to look foolish, but the sentiment was important to her. Her mother was so disappointed when she eloped; she had visions of Jeanne getting married in the gown she had saved for her.

"It's a little tight, a little yellowed, and will probably smell of mothballs, but I'll hold my breath," she laughingly remarked to Marvela and Leonard.

"She's always breathless anyway," Leonard quipped.

A gathering of over a hundred people attended the wedding. The children, grandchildren, and great-grandchildren of the bride and groom made up over a third of the attendees.

A retired Methodist minister, who lived at *Forest Glen*, performed the ceremony, and Jeanne and Leonard recited vows they had written, which included the words, "We will cherish each other every day of our lives, for as long as we are on this planet—and beyond." Ahna then played some lively music while the progeny of the two danced. The residents clapped their hands; several stood up and swayed to the music. Marvela had worn high-heeled red satin slippers, thankful she could hold on to Stan's wheelchair should she teeter or slip. She hadn't worn heels since she last wore the gown, and decided she may never wear them again. She used to love to dance, so when one of Leonard's burly sons asked her to dance, she kicked off her shoes and let him lead her around the floor.

"Thanks for holding me up." Marvela laughed when he returned her to her seat. "My balance isn't what it used to be, but it was great fun."

A gala reception was held in the beautifully decorated dining room. The champagne flowed; eloquent, and sometimes humorous toasts were proposed. Leonard's younger brother, aged eighty, made Leonard promise to name their first child for him.

Leonard's four sons, all grandfathers, sang old love songs—barbershop style. Jeanne's three beautiful daughters, all grandmothers, performed an improvised dance number. The grandchildren sang some Beatle's songs, and the four great-grandchildren recited a rap one of them had written, "Our gramps and grandma aren't only great, they're the greatest, we really rate . . .*"*

When it was all over, Stan asked Marvela to join him for a final nightcap.

After settling in Stan's living room, they shared impressions of the wedding, agreeing it was the best they had ever attended.

"I never laughed so much at a wedding. They are usually solemn affairs," Marvela giggled.

Stan confided he had a large church wedding with all of the traditional trimmings. He related that his marriage was childless, but fairly happy until his accident. His wife was sorry, but she couldn't face living with an invalid, so they divorced.

"That hurt a lot, but I've made my peace with her. You could say we're still friends," Stan said, and then added, "but not really."

Marvela told Stan about the circumstances of her divorce.

"You could say John and I are still friends, but not really." Marvela laughed.

"You didn't marry again?" Stan inquired.

"No, although there were some close calls," Marvela responded wistfully.

She had trouble getting any sleep that night. The wedding, and her conversation with Stan, brought back memories of the "close calls" she had mentioned. About a year after John moved out, she had an affair with a cameraman. They traveled together on a number of reporting assignments. Gil was married, unhappily, he said. He had two young children whom he seldom mentioned. Marvela thought, naively, that Gil might leave his wife and marry her. But this was not to be. It seemed his infatuation with Marvela coincided with their trips. They rarely saw each other while in New York. During a trip to Russia, Marvela confronted Gil about his intentions.

"I can't go on like this, Gil. It's obvious our relationship is convenient for you, but very difficult for me. I would like to marry you, but I realize this was never your intention." Marvela couldn't keep back her tears.

Gil put his arms around her, and held her close. "I do love you, Marvela, and I have thought of leaving my wife—but she's a devoted mother, and I couldn't break my kids' hearts."

They had one last bittersweet night together. Gil soon transferred to another network, and she never saw him again.

In hindsight, Marvela knew Gil, and she were not compatible enough for a remotely happy marriage. He was rarely without a cigarette; she abhorred smoking. While he said he was devoted to his children, he rarely spent time with them. Marvela loved the theater and classical music; Gil preferred science fiction books, and country western music. He couldn't be called handsome, although he had startlingly blue eyes, and a disarming, crooked grin. His offbeat charm had definitely captured her heart. He had an infectious sense of humor, and made her laugh a lot. She had trouble forgetting him.

Marvela had several suitors over the years. A close colleague of John's, who had been present at their wedding, asked her to marry him. Frederick was a good companion in many ways; they enjoyed the arts and liked to attend the theater, but there was little passion. They lived together for nearly a year after the children were grown, but never married. In some ways he reminded her of John. He even looked like him. The children didn't like him much. They thought he was too controlling; Marvela had to agree. Marie was in college and refused to come home for the holidays if he would be there. Steve and Ron got along with Frederick, but didn't want their mother to marry him. Frederick didn't seem too heartbroken when Marvela broke off their relationship. They had a fairly amicable parting of the ways.

After that Marvela gave up on dating. She liked her independence and had several close women friends in New York. Roger and his friends made sure she had an escort when one was required, so her social life didn't suffer.

One of her good friends lived in the apartment below hers. Sid Langley was a fashion model who was getting too old for the glamour shots. She did catalog work for a while, but even that was waning.

"You still look great, Sid," Marvela told her. "You're an excellent amateur photographer, why don't you try that end of the camera professionally?"

After a rough start, and near bankruptcy, Sid's new business started to flourish. The modeling agencies liked her work, and she was a natural in that world. Marvela decided to call her. It was after midnight in New York, but Sid rarely got to bed until the wee hours of the morning. Sid always let the answering machine pick up her calls; she'd respond if she wanted to talk to the caller.

"Sid, you'd better pick up that phone, it's Marvela."

"Marvela, I think our old serendipity is working," Sid finally answered. "I was about to call you. How are you doing, all settled?"

"I'm so settled, it's pathetic," Marvela replied with a laugh.

"Then you wouldn't mind a visitor?"

"I'd love it. When can you come?"

"I have a shoot scheduled in Kansas City. How does next weekend sound?"

"I can't wait. Do you want me to meet you at the airport?"

"No, that is taken cared of. I'm not a models' photographer anymore. When my daughter had her child, I switched to babies. I have a commission to photograph the mayor's newborn twin granddaughters in KC. They'll pick me up at the airport. I'll call you when I'm finished. You can pick me up there."

Marvela hardly recognized her old friend when she came bouncing out of the mayor's mansion.

"You look terrific, I like your new short hairstyle, and the auburn color looks great with your coloring."

"Thanks, friend, you look good too." Sid looked her over. "Actually those few extra pounds filled out your face."

Marvela punched Sid's arm. "I'd almost forgotten how brutally honest you can be." Sid laughed. "You do look good, Marvela, much more rested and relaxed than the last time I saw you."

"I'm sure that's true. You haven't gained an ounce of weight, but your face is amazingly free of wrinkles. What's your secret?"

"Only my plastic surgeon knows for sure." Sid winked.

"You went all the way this time?"

"Yeah, it was time, but it was more of an ordeal than I expected. I was nearly blind for three weeks, and black-and-blue for over a month," Sid grimaced.

"I'll probably live with my character lines now. I don't have the stomach, or the funds, to try to get rid of them. At my age, it's time to accept what cannot easily be changed. But you're much younger than I."

Sid put her hand on Marvela's arm. "I'll be seventy in two years."

Marvela patted her hand. "That's younger!" On the way to *Forest Glen* they chatted animatedly and giggled over good times in New York.

"Do you have a current significant other, Sid?"

"Not currently, or even immediate past," Sid replied. "Any prospects here?"

"If you want to push a wheelchair," Marvela responded with a grin. "Actually, the youngest and best-looking guy here is in a wheelchair."

"Tell me about him?" Sid asked.

Marvela told her about Stan and his accident. "We have a lot in common. He's a good friend."

"Sometimes good friends are the best marriage prospects." Sid gave her a sly look. When they arrived at *Forest Glen*, they kicked off their shoes and settled on the couch.

"This calls for a celebration, I bought some champagne." Marvela poured two glasses of the sparkling liquid.

"Your ex lives near here, doesn't he? Have you seen him?" Sid inquired as she settled back on the cushions.

"As a matter of fact, I have," Marvela replied as she filled Sid's glass. "After he was here at Thanksgiving, he called several times. He's asked me to dinner, but I have found convenient excuses not to go."

"I've never met him, you know. How about accepting his invitation, and I'll tag along," Sid suggested with a mischievous grin.

Marvela emptied her glass before replying. "Not a bad idea. Let's do it. I'll call him right now."

John was a bit taken aback about Marvela's suggestion that he take two women to dinner, but replied gallantly.

"How could I refuse two beautiful women?"

The dinner was a success. It was obvious that John was impressed by Sid. Marvela hadn't seen him so animated since the first years of their marriage.

"You didn't tell me how handsome John is," Sid chided when they got back to the apartment.

"Yes, he's aged well." Marvela felt a small tinge of jealousy. "He was certainly attracted to you."

"Hey, friend, I don't want to spoil anything between you two."

"Sid, there's nothing between us, well maybe some shared memories—not all of them pleasant." Marvela hugged her friend.

At dinner that evening Marvela and Sid shared a table with Jeanne and Leonard. Stan was in Washington. Marvela also introduced Sid to several other residents she had come to know through the writing group.

"What delightful people," Sid remarked when they got back to the apartment. "I'll bet there's a wealth of fascinating stories, just waiting to be revealed."

"I've heard a few, and they are remarkable. I've thought of writing up some living histories for my writing class."

"A great idea," Sid continued, "Those faces! I'd love to photograph some of them."

"Why don't you? I could compile their stories, and you could illustrate them." Marvela found herself getting excited about the project.

Sid was equally enthused. "If you'll put up with me for another week or so, I'll start the photography end of it."

Marvela told Kyle about their ideas. He was enthusiastic and encouraged them to get started. He gave them names of some residents whom he thought had interesting stories to tell.

CHAPTER EIGHT

Sid and Marvela started their living history project by interviewing Henry Hickson, a World War II veteran who had been captured by the Germans. His story had them spellbound. He was a bomber pilot who had been shot down over occupied France. Members of the French resistance hid him, but the Germans knew where he was. They had seen him parachute out of his plane, and kept a close surveillance on his whereabouts, hoping to capture members of the resistance along with Henry.

"Are you going to tell me that the Germans killed your French benefactors?" Marvela asked, taking notes as rapidly as possible, while Sid was getting candid shots of Henry.

"Amazingly, they didn't," Henry explained. "The man and wife who rescued me had just left to go on another secret mission, when the German soldiers came to raid the place. After I was captured they questioned me for four days and nights about the whereabouts of the French couple. They gave me water to drink, but no food. I was roughed up as well, but not severely tortured. They finally gave up on trying to obtain information which they didn't really believe I had. I was transported by truck, with two other prisoners, to the infamous Stalag-Luft IV in Germany. There we were stripped, searched, and knocked around. A big, burly guard landed several well-placed blows on my body until the captain of the guards stopped him."

"How terrible," Marvela exclaimed. "You could have been killed."

"Yeah, I was badly bruised, and I have no hearing in my left ear due to his cuffing. You can believe, I vowed to stay away from him."

"Did you have enough food to eat?"

"Thin potato soup was our usual fare. Each day we were given two loaves of black bread, three if we were lucky, to divide among the eight of us in the cell."

"Did that cause some fights among you?"

"No, we developed a pretty fair system for sharing. In fact, one buddy gave me his share, when I was sick with dysentery."

"That brings us to sanitation."

"Pretty primitive. We had to dig our own latrines. Not so good on winter days."

"How did you stay warm?"

"There was a small wood stove, but sometimes no wood. We were each given a rough German blanket. Thank goodness we got some supplies, including blankets, from the Red Cross, but we were always cold in winter and hot in summer."

"How did you spend your days?"

"Hardship breeds ingenuity. We used any scraps of paper we could find to make playing cards. We played every card game known to man. We got occasional cigarette rations. Since I didn't smoke, I traded my cigarette rations for food, or things like paper and pencils from the German soldiers."

"How long were you a prisoner?"

"Two very long years. There were times when I was so cold, hungry, and sick, I almost gave up. But thoughts of my sweetheart, now my wife, kept me going. I wrote to her whenever it was possible, and three letters from her came through the Red Cross."

"How did your ordeal end?"

"When the Germans knew they were losing the war, we were forced to march to Berlin. It was a very long, hard march, and we lost a lot of men on the way. Fortunately, it was summer, and we were able to find some leftover grain in the fields, and sometimes fruit on trees. The German soldiers demanded food from farmers, and usually gave us small portions. By that time, some of the German guards had become quite friendly. We slept on the ground, or in haylofts. Some American soldiers on trucks met us, when we were nearing the city. They gave us rides, and the first chocolate bars I had seen in years."

Henry pulled out a picture. "One of the GI's took this picture. I'm the skeleton on the left."

Marvela looked shocked.

"You'd never believe it to look at me now. I married my high school sweetheart, and she turned out to be a great cook. Now I blame the chef at *Forest Glen*," he laughed. Sid told him he looked great, and offered to give him copies of the pictures she had taken. Henry was quite photogenic. He had thick, wavy gray hair, bushy eyebrows, and an aquiline nose.

"What a story!" Sid exclaimed after the interview. Who will you interview next?"

"A holocaust victim. Ruth told me about her. Esther is ninety and quite articulate. She was a young adult, when she was taken to the concentration camps. Her story parallels Anne Frank's, except she was kept hidden for a year in Poland. She was a friend to the daughters of a well-to-do Polish Gentile family—the Petrovski's. When the German soldiers came for Esther's parents, she was visiting the Petrovskis. In an attempt to keep Esther safe, they hid her in a cave underneath their kitchen for a year."

"What a story. Will she let us interview her?" Sid asked.

"We'll need to go to Esther's apartment for the interview. She is often bedridden now, but she has a companion living with her, who brings her food from the dining room and sees to her general comfort," Marvela informed Sid.

"Will she mind having her picture taken?" Sid inquired.

"I don't think so. She wears a becoming wig and always looks nice," Marvela replied. They found Esther looking spry and in a talkative mood.

"I'll show you my number, so you'll know vhat I tell you is true." She raised her sleeve and revealed a fading set of blue inked numbers. "They are always there reminding me of a time I'd like to forget." She spoke with a heavy accent. "But I vill tell you my story, Marvela. First tell me about your friend."

Marvela introduced Sid and asked if it would be all right if they took some pictures.

"Ach, yes. I had Gilda get my cosmetic case, so I could vear a little makeup." She laughed. "Not that it does much goot at my age." Sid assured her she looked great.

"Vell, Marvela, vhere vould you like to begin?"

"I told Sid about your hiding place at the Petrovskis. How did the Germans find you?"

"Mrs. Petrovski hid me in the cave. Her husband fled Poland to go to England before the Germans came. He had a Jewish grandmother, so he vas at risk. Also, he vanted to join the Allied fighting forces. Mrs. Petrovski stayed in Varsaw to take care of her tree teenage girls who were in school. Vhen she heard zat her mother was dying in Gdansk, she took the girls and vent to her. She left me a month's supply of food and vasser, tinking she vould be back before then. I kept track of the days on my calendar. Six veeks had already passed, and I vas out of food and vasser, so I took my flashlight and vent upstairs to get some vasser and look for food. I only shone the flashlight one time, but a passing German patrol saw it and knocked on the door. I fled back to the cave, but zey came looking the next day and found me."

"I vas blonde and blue-eyed, so the German soldiers veren't sure I vas Jewish. But zey looked up the records, and found verification. One of the soldiers kept making passes at me, but his officer made him stop. I tink he vas a kind man." Esther paused and blew her nose.

"You were taken to Auschwitz, weren't you?" Marvela asked gently.

"Yes," her voice shook. "I vas dere about a year before the American soldiers came. Just in time, for I vas to be taken to the gas chambers the next day. Marvela, I can't go on now, maybe I can talk more about it later." She was trembling; her concerned companion added a blanket and tucked her in.

Marvela went over to the bed. "Esther, thank you for talking to us. We don't want to stir up bad memories. You rest now." Marvela kissed her forehead.

"Ve'll talk more another time." Esther gave a little wave and closed her eyes.

"It's still fresh in her mind after nearly seventy years," Sid commented. "The suffering was unimaginable," her voice choked. "Shall we call it a day? Maybe we can do some upbeat interviews tomorrow."

"I have a doozie lined up," Marvela chuckled. "Everyone calls her Bubbles, but that isn't her real name—which she won't reveal, along with her age. She asked us to come to her apartment because she has a lot to show us there."

Bubbles greeted them dressed in a short, bright blue-sequined dress with a pink feather boa around her neck. A rhinestone headband with a pink feather circled shiny platinum-blonde hair. She had a long cigarette holder in her mouth; she was heavily made-up complete with artificial eyelashes.

"Not to worry, Marvela, it's not lit," she laughed and fluffed her hair, "and this is a wig, of course. Marvela, you know I have white hair and use very little make-up, but I want you to see the 'Ziegfield Girl!'"

"Bubbles, I haven't told Sid anything about your past, so start wherever you want to." After Sid was introduced, she started snapping pictures. Bubbles favored her with some provocative poses before she started telling her story.

"I was born in St. Louis. I had a burning desire to be a Broadway star since I was about four years old. I begged my parents for singing and dancing lessons, and doting parents that they were they started me in lessons when I was five. I had the lead in several high school plays and musicals, and thought I was ready for the big white way. At that time, auditions were held in many major cities of the country for chorus roles in the Ziegfield Follies. I was accepted when I was barely fifteen and had one year under the direction of Florenz Ziegfield."

"You were terribly young to be in New York by yourself," Marvela commented.

"Oh, I wasn't alone, my mother went to New York with me in 1930, and stayed with me for five years. So you see I was well-chaperoned, even though it meant the end of my parents' marriage."

"It seems I recall that 1931 was the last year the Follies were really big," Sid interjected.

"You're right. That year I danced in the chorus with Barbara Stanwyck and Paulette Goddard, and others you may have heard of. It was a fantastic time. Unfortunately, Florenz Ziegfield died in 1932. His second wife Billie Burke took over the Follies, but they didn't do very well after Florenz's death. I danced in the chorus until 1936 when I went to Hollywood for a bit part in the movie *The Great Ziegfield*. Would you like to see some signed photos from my Ziegfield days?" She led them into her study; the walls were covered with autographed pictures.

"Look, there's Will Rogers, and it's signed, *An Admirer.* Were you . . . ?" Marvela asked with a wink.

"Oh no, but he did take me to dinner once—along with five other chorus girls. By that time, 1934, he was a popular Hollywood star. He came to see the Follies when he was in New York. You know he was a star of the Follies in its heyday during the late 1920s. Everyone was devastated when he was killed in a plane crash in Alaska in 1935.

"I'm a great admirer of Will Rogers. His homespun philosophy and humor never gets old," Marvela said.

"Hey, who have we here?" Sid inquired as she pointed to another photograph.

"I treasure this picture of Dick Powell. I really had a crush on him. Remember he played the part of Florenz Ziegfield in the 1936 movie *The Great Ziegfield.* Sometimes I regret not staying in Hollywood, but my mother thought there were too many temptations there."

"William Powell's picture is signed *To my love.* Was he one of the temptations?" Sid asked with raised eyebrows.

"I'm not talking." Bubbles giggled. "I went back to St. Louis after my Hollywood experience and married my high school sweetheart. He courted me the whole time I was in New York. It's a good thing he was a rich banker's son, for he became a regular stage door Johnny. Coincidentally, Johnny was his name. He traveled to New York several times a month. My dressing room looked like a flower shop." Bubbles laughed.

"So did you marry him?" Marvela asked.

"Yes, I became a banker's wife, and led a very respectable social life in St. Louis. Johnny and I raised a daughter and two wonderful sons. One of them is a lawyer in Kansas City; that's why I chose *Forest Glen*. Johnny died quite suddenly twenty years ago." Bubbles took off her wig, fluffed her hair and pulled out some scrapbooks. "These pictures and clippings tell the whole story."

"Could I borrow them? They'll help a lot when I write this up," Marvela asked. "I promise to take good care of them."

"I trust you, Marvela. You are such a great addition to *Forest Glen*. I hope we'll become good friends. Maybe we can cook up some entertainment that will knock the socks off of some of these stodgy people." Bubbles chuckled. "I can still do the Charleston, as long as I know there's someone to pick me up should I fall."

Back at Marvela's apartment, Sid asked, "How old do you think she is? She's certainly kept a slim figure, and her face, though lined, has beautiful bone structure."

"If she went to the Follies in 1930 at age fifteen, she's got to be at least ninety or more. It's hard to believe, for she's one of the 'overqualified' ones around here, able to get about quite well without help; although once at dinner she confided she had some heart problems."

After a leisurely cup of coffee, Sid asked, "May I check my e-mail? Time to catch up on things at home."

After reading her e-mail Sid said with regret, "So sorry, partner, but I have to leave early. I sent some of my baby pictures to a publisher, and they're very interested in developing a book. They set up an appointment for day after tomorrow."

"That's wonderful, Sid. Your pictures are amazingly creative. They'll make a great book. I'll write up the interviews I have. Together with your pictures, we should get a good spread in *Active Aging*. That should please the interviewees. Hopefully you'll come back soon. By then I'll have more interesting characters lined up. There's a World War II veteran who survived the Bataan march, and one that survived Pearl Harbor. Gilda, Esther's companion, told me of a World War II nurse who was stationed in Germany. She visited Buchenwald right after the surrender. Some of the prisoners had not yet been evacuated, and there were still corpses stacked like cordwood. Gilda also said something about an unbelievable wartime romance."

"I think she'll be another winner." Sid hugged Marvela.

"Please come back soon. I think we've just begun to find the treasures here. I'm told there are a number of musicians who played with major symphonies, and someone said there's an opera star here. She's a recluse, but maybe I can win her over."

"I'm betting that you can," Sid said as she kissed Marvela's cheek. "I've had a fascinating time, and you can be sure I'll be back."

CHAPTER NINE

Marvela was lonely after Sid left. Stan was in Washington, and Jeanne and Leonard were visiting their children. Gilda came by one morning to tell her that Esther wanted to share more of her story with her.

"Esther is feeling much better. I have been pushing her around in her wheelchair, and she would like to come by this morning if it would work for you," Gilda inquired.

"Do bring her over. I am delighted she is feeling so spry," Marvela responded. "I'll have tea ready."

Gilda and Esther came to Marvela's apartment within fifteen minutes. Marvela hugged Esther. "It's so good to see you looking so well."

"I received vord that my son and his family are coming to visit me next veek from France. Such news brightens my spirits," she said with a wide smile. "I haven't seen my two granddaughters in over four years. They are both married now. Esthermarie has a four-year-old-son I haf never seen. They are all coming, even the husbands."

"The thought of seeing our loved ones is a great energizer." Marvela smiled. "I'm so happy for you." Marvela went to the kitchen and brought out tea and peppernuts.

"Ach, my favorite little cookie. Did you bake them?" Esther asked.

"Oh no, Jeanne found them in a German specialty shop," Marvela replied.

"My husband had Russian-German ancestors, but he vasn't Jewish. My mother-in-law alvays baked pfeffernüesse at Christmastime. I kept up the tradition after she died." Esther smiled in remembrance.

"I'm curious, how did you meet your husband?" Marvela inquired.

"Vould you believe at a synagogue in Chicago? He and some friends visited several times. He vas doing a paper on comparative religions for a college class. I tink he came back more times than necessary. My girlfriends told me he couldn't keep his eyes off of me." She shook her head. "After the third visit, he boldly came up to me, and asked to take me to dinner. Vell, one thing led to another, and ve married a year later."

"And how many children did you have?" Marvela asked.

"Only one son. My husband vas a professor of French at Chicago University. My son, Villiam, majored in French. He visited France after he graduated, and stayed on to vork for various American corporations as an interpreter."

"I can understand why you are so eager for his visit. I hope I will get to meet them."

"Ve'll make sure of that." Esther nodded at Gilda.

"Gilda tells me you would like to share more of your story."

"Yes, I vanted to tell you that I vent to Poland tventy years ago, and vas able to see the Petrovskis. Ve had a very emotional reunion. My friend Svetlana was a proud grandmother—ten grandchildren. Sadly, Mr. Petrovsky died in the var. Mrs. Petrovsky was very frail vhen I vas dere, and she died several months after my visit. Svetlana is now old like me, but ve still keep in touch."

After they finished their tea and peppernuts, Marvela saw them to the door. "I hope this is the first of many more visits," Marvela said as she kissed Esther on the cheek.

When the phone rang early the next morning she answered eagerly, thinking it was probably Sid. "This is Marvela," she answered.

"Marvela, this is a voice from your past, one you didn't think you'd ever hear from again." The male voice was hoarse and weak.

"You'll have to give me a better clue," Marvela said, puzzled.

"OK, think of a habit you—" the voice faded, "dis—" There was a strangled cough.

"Gil, could it be you?"

"The one and only," he croaked.

"Where are you?"

"Probably less than an hour from you," he replied. "I'm at the Kansas University Medical Center, waiting for lung surgery." There was a fit of coughing before he continued. "I found your name in the phone book. I may not make it, but I wanted you to know I haven't forgotten you," he rasped. "Oh, oh, the men in white coats have come to take me to the operating room. I've got to hang up now, time to go. Wish me luck."

Marvela was stunned. He was right; she didn't expect to hear from him again. Gil was part of her life she didn't want to remember. Evidently his incessant smoking habit had resulted in the inevitable.

She had trouble sleeping that night. Thoughts of Gil spilled over into her dreams. In it, they were both young and vital, laughing at a story he was telling. He was driving, too fast as usual, when they rounded a sharp curve in the mountains. He lost control and the car tumbled down a cliff. She woke up in a cold sweat, turned on the light, and noted it was four in the morning. She couldn't sleep after that, her mind in turmoil. Should she call the hospital and find out if Gil survived? She wondered if any of his family was with him. She got up at six o'clock, fixed a cup of coffee, and decided to look up the number of the hospital. She was connected to the nurse's station in surgery.

"I'm calling about Gil Foster. He had lung surgery yesterday. Could you give me some information about his condition?"

"Just a minute, please. Are you a relative?"

"No, just a friend." Marvela was kept on hold for several minutes.

"Mr. Foster is in serious condition, and may not recover. We'd like to notify a next of kin, but he didn't leave any information. Could you provide a contact number?"

"No, I'm sorry. I haven't seen Gil—Mr. Foster—for about thirty years. But I'll, I'll keep checking on his condition," Marvela said, with some hesitation.

"Would you leave your number? We will need to contact someone, should he not recover," the nurse persisted.

Marvela wavered. "Well, I—I," she paused. "OK." She gave her name and phone number.

She spent most of that day trying to track down someone who could give her information about Gil or his family. She finally reached a retired coworker who had been a friend of Gil's.

"Hi, Bill. I'm so glad I reached you. I'm trying to get some information about Gil Foster. Have you kept in touch?"

"Hi Marvela, it's been a long time. The last I knew of Gil, he had divorced his first wife, remarried, and moved to Los Angeles. I haven't heard from him in at least a dozen years."

Marvela told him about Gil's current situation. "Do you have any idea how his children might be reached?"

"Sure don't. Sorry I can't be of more help. Please give my regards to Gil when you see him."

Marvela called the hospital that evening. She was connected to Gil's nurse in intensive care. "Mr. Foster is able to breathe on his own for longer periods of time. His chances of recovery have increased. If he continues to improve he may have visitors in a few days." Marvela was still conflicted about the wisdom of renewing any contact with Gil, but he seemed to be so pitifully alone.

She was glad for the opportunity to keep busy for the next few days. Jane had asked her to help plan a Valentine's celebration for the residents.

"I'd like to honor the couples who have been married over sixty years," Jane informed Marvela. "Actually there are two couples here who have been married over seventy years. One of the husbands is in assisted living, and one in nursing care, but I think they'll be able to come to the dinner. The wives are still in Independent Living or were the last time I checked."

The two women enlisted the help of Kyle and his staff in planning the festivities. The string quartet that played for Jeanne and Leonard's wedding was asked to play old love songs for a sing-along. Marvela developed a power point presentation incorporating the lyrics with appropriate illustrations. After a delicious dinner she interviewed the couples to be honored, and asked them the secrets of their lasting marriages.

"We never went to bed mad," one wife commented. "The rule was to kiss and make up before we went to sleep."

One husband joked, "It's a give-and-take proposition. When I give, she takes, and when she gives, I ask her if she's feeling OK."

His wife laughed. "He makes me laugh. I guess that's why I stayed with him."

The festive dinner was well received by the residents. Jane and her helpers created table decorations that looked professional. They departed from the usual red and white, instead incorporated rainbow colors in the flower arrangements, which featured glittering white Cupids in a variety of poses. Grandma Layton posters were given as door prizes.

Jane told Marvela about Grandma Layton, a native of Kansas whose drawings are now world-renowned.

"It's difficult to explain the work of Elizabeth 'Grandma' Layton. She started drawing at age sixty-seven using the contour method," Jane said.

"Is that where a person looks in the mirror and draws whatever she sees?" Marvela queried, remembering some art classes she took in college.

"That's right, and Grandma Layton drew herself, wrinkles, age spots, warts, and all." Jane chuckled and continued. "Her drawing actually healed her of a lifelong depression. They expressed her social consciousness and deep, often dark aspects of life, such as the death of a child, fear, loneliness, the often harrowing duties of being a woman, and the need for love and romance."

"So her drawings actually portray 'every woman' in a way?"

"They do. I have several of her posters, and I relate to all of them," Jane responded. "She wrote a wonderful piece on wrinkles to go with her drawing entitled 'Masks,'" Jane continued. "I think of it when I start to feel depressed about the many lines on my face. Grandma Layton said, 'Say you're real happy for a minute, and you put on that mask, and that's going to make an indentation in those muscles to a certain extent.'"

"There's little doubt that most of your lines were formed from laughter," Marvela commented.

"And forgetting to wear sunscreen," Jane added.

A heavy snow fell that night, so Marvela postponed her tentative plans to go see Gil. She called the hospital and was told he was making a recovery, but was very weak and still in intensive care. So she curled up with a good book, choosing to stay in her apartment all day, munching on snacks, not bothering to get dressed or go to the dining room. She welcomed a call from Marie. Marvela didn't tell her about Gil, a part of her life she had never shared with her daughter.

"Mom, you'd better make your plane reservations. May twenty is the big day!" Marie enthused.

"A May wedding will be special. I'll search the Internet for the best travel deal. You know your father suggested we go to the wedding together."

"Yes, he told me. I think it would be great. I'm so glad you two have reconciled." "I, too, am pleased," Marvela conceded. "It's like turning on a light in a room that has been dark too long."

"Beautifully stated, Mom. It has lightened my spirits as well," Marie confided. "I so want all of my family to be at the wedding. We will invite over a hundred of Nigel's relatives and old friends, so having my family represented is really important to me."

"You can be assured I'll be there with bells on, and I'll do all I can to convince Ron and Steve to attend," Marvela assured her. "I guess I'll have to shop for a hat?"

"Oh yes, a hat is a must. You might want to wait until you get here though, there are so many more 'fitting' choices," Marie laughed.

"I haven't bought a hat since I was first married. I'm not a hat person, so finding a 'fitting' one might not be easy."

"Shopping for one will be fun, Mom."

"Doing anything with you will be fun." As always Marvela's spirits lifted when she talked with her daughter.

She awoke to sunshine the next morning. It might be a good day to visit Gil. After checking on the road conditions, and finding them cleared, she put on black wool slacks and a turquoise sweater. Like John, Gil liked to see her in turquoise. As she put on some turquoise earrings, she laughed at herself in the mirror, admitting to her vanity, a little vexed that she still wanted to please men.

Gil remained in the intensive care unit. The nurse told her she could visit him, but no longer than fifteen minutes. She was led to a small cubicle.

Gil's eyes were closed, so she studied his face for a minute before speaking. She wouldn't have recognized him. He had long, tangled gray hair and a beard; his face was skeletal, his breathing labored.

Before she could speak, he opened his eyes and gazed at her for a while before saying weakly, "You came."

She went over to the bed and took his hand. "I guess I couldn't have not come." She smiled. "You sounded like you needed a friend."

He managed a faint smile. "Can't believe you would—" he swallowed, "still be one." There was a long pause before Marvela spoke. "I called your old friend Bill. He told me a little about your life, but said he hadn't heard from you in years. He sent his regards."

Gil spoke haltingly. "So you know . . . I left Ann . . . and married Lola."

Marvela nodded.

"Lola died . . . of an overdose . . . three years ago. Haven't seen . . . my kids since . . . I left Ann."

"What brought you to Kansas City?" Marvela inquired.

"Got a job . . . at a television station . . . here." Gil started to cough.

The nurse came in and motioned for Marvela to leave.

"Please come back," Gil pleaded in a surprisingly strong voice.

"I'll try." Marvela stepped out of the room. She stopped at the cafeteria for a cup of coffee.

The only thing she felt for Gil was pity. She'd visit him again, but would make sure he didn't become dependent on her. He had been a part of her life, when she was footloose but not fancy free. Her job then, and the travel it involved, seemed to cut her free from her moorings. Was she ever really that emotionally needy? She had reflected at length on that time of her life. Over time, she forgave herself for conduct, which was not a part of her authentic self.

Marvela was cutting and pasting a mock-up copy of the newsletter when the phone rang.

"Hi, Marvela, it's Gil. I'm out of intensive care, and there's an empty chair in my room."

"Gil, I'm pleased you are doing well. I'll try to get up there tomorrow. I've been involved in a project that has kept me very busy."

"You always were an intense one when it came to work, but I thought you were retired."

"Recycled might be a better word." Marvela laughed. "Admittedly my pace is slower, but as always, I need a creative outlet."

"Creative outlets aren't in my immediate future," Gil commented. "But I could use some decent reading material. Old issues of *People Magazine,* just don't cut it for me."

On her way to the hospital, Marvela stopped at a bookstore and picked up some magazines and books she thought Gil would like. She remembered he liked science fiction. When she arrived at Gil's hospital room, she was surprised to see him looking so well. His hair had been cut and combed, and his beard trimmed. He was hooked up to only one IV tube.

"Hey, you've made progress," Marvela said cheerfully as she dropped the reading material on his bedside table.

Gil grabbed her arm and squeezed it, "Do you have any idea how much this means to me? Please sit down and tell me about your life?"

They chatted for a while, catching up on major events in their lives.

"You still look great, Marvela. The years have been good to you. That's more than I can say for myself." Gil shook his head. "I owe so many people apologies, including you." He looked at her appealingly, his eyes filled with remorse.

"I've never been one to dwell on the past, and I don't intend to start, so forget any apologies to me," Marvela said kindly. "But I do wonder about your children. Wouldn't you like to contact them?"

"I would, very much, but I don't even know where to start," Gil replied with tears in his eyes.

"Why don't you give me their names and the most recent addresses you have. I'll do a computer search for you," Marvela offered.

"They may not want to see me, but I do want to give it a try." Gil reached for Marvela's hand. "You are just too good."

"Not to be trite, but blood is thicker than water. I can't believe they wouldn't want to see you," Marvela said sincerely.

As she drove back to *Forest Glen*, Marvela wondered about Gil's children, and the relationships to their father. From what she gathered from the information he gave her, he had severed all contacts when he left Ann.

She decided to use a paid search since she had so little information about the children's current whereabouts. They undoubtedly had married by now and had children of their own. The son was easiest to find since he had the same last name. She found five Zachary Fosters at different addresses and decided to contact all of them. She had e-mail addresses for three of them, so she sent messages inquiring if they had a father named Gil Foster who used to work for ABC. She wrote letters to the other two. She got an immediate response from two of the e-mails stating Gil was not the name of their father. Five days passed before she heard from the third: *Gil Foster was my father's name. Who is inquiring, please?*

Marvela responded:

I am a friend of Gil Foster's. He is recovering from life—threatening surgery, and would like to get in touch with his children. You may e-mail me, and I will pass any information on to Gil who is in a hospital in Kansas City.

Marvela decided she would wait for a reply before contacting Gil. She heard from Zachary the next day.

I have mixed feeling about seeing my dad, but you may give him my address and phone number. I have two grown sons, and I would not ever want to be alienated from them, so I have more compassion now than I would have twenty years ago. My wife died of cancer three years ago, so I'm no stranger to despair. He added his address and phone number.

Marvela called Gil and read him the e-mail.

"I'll call him immediately. Poor Zach, he was such a good kid. To think I'm the grandfather of grown grandsons. Marvela, where has the time gone, and how can I ever make up even a fraction of it?" Gil was sobbing.

"You've made a start, Gil. I commend you for that. Let me know how things turn out with Zachary."

CHAPTER TEN

Marvela waited a week before going back to see Gil. When she entered his room, he was sitting in a recliner. His beard had been shaved, and he'd put on some weight. He smiled at her and reached out his hand.

"What a difference a week makes," Marvela said as she shook Gil's hand. "I think you must have some good news to share."

"You bet I do. Zachary lives in St. Louis. He drove here yesterday. We had a real man-to-man talk. I think he has forgiven me, Marvela. He gave me his sister's phone number in New York City, but cautioned me not to expect much cordiality. He was right. Annemarie started crying as soon as I gave my name. She told me to call her again in a week. By that time she'd probably know if she wanted to talk to me. I plan to call her tomorrow. Any words of wisdom?"

"Don't rush her, even if she keeps you waiting another month or longer," Marvela advised. "Will you be seeing Zachary again?"

"Oh yeah. He's coming next Sunday and bringing the boys. One of them is married and his wife is expecting a child. Imagine me a great-grandfather!"

Marvela proceeded hesitantly. "Is your ex wife . . . is Ann still living?"

"She lives with Annemarie in New York. Annemarie is an up-and-coming fashion designer, twice divorced. Zachary says Ann is in good health."

Marvela rose to leave. "Gil, I hope the same will be said of you very soon."

"You're coming back, aren't you?" Gil asked with concern.

"Probably not, Gil. I think you will soon have the support of your family. I'm pleased I could be your friend when you needed one."

"But, but I thought we . . ."

Marvela put a hand over his mouth, kissed him on the forehead and walked out.

The phone was ringing when she got back to her apartment.

"Hi, Marvela, long time no see."

"Right, John. I left a message on your machine over a week ago, but didn't get a return call," Marvela said briskly.

"I've been traveling and just got back last night. I spent some time with my mother on her one hundredth birthday. She's in a nursing home in Ohio. She can't walk, but is fairly astute mentally. She has some memory lapses, but we were able to reminisce and look through old photo albums."

"Stella always was a trouper," Marvela said. "I remember her being depressed for a while after your father died of a stroke, in his late sixties, I believe."

"Yes, it took her awhile to get over that, but she is a strong woman. After several indecisive months she recovered, and ran the family dairy farm for many years," John said.

"She asked about you, Marvela. You know she didn't get along with Elaine. Probably because she couldn't let go of the hope we would get back together," John mused.

"Did you go on to New York after visiting in Ohio?" Marvela asked, wanting to change the subject.

"I did, I looked up some old friends and colleagues," John responded.

"Anybody I know?"

"Most of my old colleagues at NYU are retired and live elsewhere—or died. I did look in on Frederick, but he didn't remember me. Sadly, he's in a care home for Alzheimer's patients."

"I'm sorry to hear that. Frederick was a good friend," Marvela said. "Didn't he marry your old secretary a few years back?"

"He did. She was visiting Frederick when I was there, and seems quite devoted to him."

"I had dinner with Sid. She sends her greetings. Her baby picture book has just been published to rave reviews."

Marvela swallowed, "She left a short message on my answering machine several weeks ago. I called her back, but she hasn't responded. No doubt she's been very busy." A note of sarcasm crept into Marvela's voice.

John chuckled. "That she has. By the way, I checked flight schedules during some of my downtime. United has some really good fares to London. You might check them out and see what you think."

"I'll do that. However I plan to go to London at least three weeks before the wedding, maybe a month. That may be too early for you," Marvela responded curtly. "I really need to go, I'll talk to you later."

"Whoa, not so fast. What's bothering you, Marvela?"

"Sorry, John, this has been a rather hectic time for me," Marvela responded with a hint of contrition.

"I can understand that you want to go to London early, but maybe we can reach a compromise. Think about it, will you?" John asked gently.

"I'll do that, John, and I promise to get back to you soon," Marvela responded, with some warmth in her voice.

After Marvela hung up, she decided to call Sid. She was obviously harboring some ill will, and she didn't like it one bit.

Surprisingly Sid answered on the first ring, "Marvela, how good to hear your voice. You've been on my mind a lot lately. I apologize for not persisting in reaching you."

"That's OK, Sid. John tells me you've been extremely busy," Marvela said, trying to keep her voice friendly.

"John and I had dinner, and a nice visit. I assure you, that's all. We talked about you a lot," Sid paused before saying, "I think John is still in love with you. Any chance of you two getting back together?"

Marvela gave a sigh of relief. "Sid, you know me like a book. I guess I still have some underlying feelings for John—first love, and all that, but I don't have any conscious desire to get back with him."

"He's very lonely. You know he's the marrying kind," Sid said seriously.

Marvela laughed. "That's why I thought he was interested in you."

"Marvela Higglesford, you know I'm not the marrying kind," Sid responded vehemently. "After the father of my daughter wouldn't marry me, I gave up on that institution."

"I suppose I did also, after John left me," Marvela hesitated, "By the way I saw Gil."

"No kidding. Tell me all about it," Sid's voice was full of curiosity.

Marvela related the circumstances of her recent involvement with Gil.

"You certainly were kind to him, but I think you were wise in cutting it off as you did," Sid commented.

"Well, it wasn't difficult. There are no underlying feelings there," Marvela said with finality.

"As usual, friend, it's great to talk with you," Sid said warmly. "I'll probably be coming to Kansas City on a book tour some time soon. You can be sure we'll get together."

"I'm looking forward to it," Marvela responded with equal warmth.

Calling Sid was a good idea, Marvela thought. *I feel so much better now*. She got on the Internet and checked flight schedules. John was right, United offered the best fares. She called Marie, and they discussed Marvela's arrival time.

"If you and dad would come two weeks before the wedding, you could help with last minute chores," Marie suggested. "Actually, Nigel's three sisters are more than eager to help, so two weeks ought to be about right for you guys."

Marvela called John to relay Marie's suggestion.

"Sounds good to me," John chuckled. "Marie's wish is our command. I'll order the tickets and send you a bill for your half, if that's OK. Better yet, let's have dinner and talk over the details. How about Friday night, I'll pick you up."

Marvela agreed to his suggestion with little hesitation. "I'll be ready at seven." They had a cordial dinner; most of it spent discussing an appropriate wedding gift for Marie. They decided to ask her for a wish list, discarding the option of simply giving her money.

Time passed rapidly for Marvela. The *Forest Glen* Newsletter took a lot of her time. She also had doctors' appointments. After the results of the lab tests were in, Dr. Peterson declared her quite healthy. She was pleased with her new doctor. While not a holistic practitioner, he seemed to be open-minded about complimentary medical practices. When she told him she was grateful for good health at her age, he retorted, "Marvela, chronological age is just a number. Your biological age is the number that counts."

She liked the concept "age is just a number."

She had had two breast biopsies, so annual mammograms and self-examinations were essential. Her bone scan showed improvement in her bone density, although she had to continue taking bone strengthening medication. The ophthalmologist said she had the beginnings of cataracts, which he would watch, but there was no need for surgery at this time.

Marvela considered herself fortunate and vowed to be religious about following preventive measures. She'd taken vitamin supplements all her life. She also followed energy medicine practices she had learned in several workshops. This entailed exercises like tracing meridians, cross-patterning, and various therapeutic postures. Most medical doctors scoffed at these procedures and the theories behind them, but Marvela had sought the advice of holistic medical doctors who encouraged her in these pursuits. She'd undergone cytotoxic tests to determine any food allergies; thank goodness there were no serious ones. She followed a Mediterranean diet as much as possible, although it was difficult to do at *Forest Glen*—the rich desserts were hard to resist. She wasn't a vegetarian, but didn't eat much meat. Sweets usually weren't a problem, although she indulged on occasion. Her willpower failed when there were salted nuts in the cupboard, so she rarely bought them.

Marvela's life at *Forest Glen* had settled into a comfortable routine. She was involved in enough activities to ward off boredom. While the newsletter took up a lot of time, she still found time for reading and attending aqua aerobics classes fairly regularly, although there were days she didn't feel up to the organized classes. The small talk and outright gossip some of the participants engaged in turned her off. She felt like an outsider, since most of the women had been together for several years, and they seemed comfortable with each other. She admonished herself to relax and enjoy the exercise.

She enjoyed the writing group, although she sometimes got a bit irritated at some of the members whom she thought had provincial views. She felt some of them probably thought she was too progressive, and maybe even too talented. The writing she shared included poetry, and short stories. Mainly she was trying different creative outlets and was hoping for support and verbal approval, but she received few compliments. Usually she laughed at herself for such adolescent-like needs. By and large the group was fun, and she would often tell herself to lighten up and enjoy the camaraderie. She was aware that the East Coast sophistication she was accustomed to often was not genuine. No matter one's age and experience, life always presented opportunities to learn valuable lessons. She definitely wanted to keep open to new experiences and different lifestyles.

One night at dinner, the hostess asked Marvela if she would like to share a table with an attractive gray blonde woman who had been ushered in just ahead of her. Stan was in Washington and Jeanne and Leonard were eating out that night. After the women were seated they introduced themselves. It didn't take long for Marvela to determine that Della Stewart was the World War II nurse Gilda had mentioned.

"I am delighted to meet you, Marvela. I've wanted to tell you how much I enjoy the newsletters," Della said enthusiastically.

"Thank you Della. I, too, wanted to meet you. I've heard a bit about your experiences in World War II, and I've been hoping to interview you. My photographer friend from New York visits me occasionally, and we're working on a project involving *Forest Glen* residents who have fascinating stories to tell. She takes photographs, and I write up the interviews."

"What a fascinating venture. I will be happy to give you a copy of the memoirs I wrote. They pretty well detail my wartime experiences as a nurse. Now I am interested in your story. I've heard by the grapevine that you were a TV producer in New York. I'd love to hear more about that time of your life."

Marvela told her a little about her New York days. Della was full of questions. Marvela wanted to hear more about Della's past; it wasn't easy to get her to talk about herself.

"Della, I understand you had a rather spectacular wartime romance that evolved into marriage. Would you tell me about it?" Marvela asked as Della reached for her water.

"OK, this story I love to relate," she smiled. "I first met Robert when I was stationed in England. We met at a dance, well, I danced and he watched." She laughed. "He was an RAF pilot, and was recovering from a broken foot. Our eyes met, literally across the crowded room. He hobbled over and bought me a drink. We talked for hours, but it was wartime, and I didn't think I would see him again."

"But you did," Marvela inserted.

"Yes, it was when I was stationed in Stuttgart, Germany. One day I had some time off and I decided to take a stroll in the countryside. It was really off limits, but I felt the need to be alone for a while. The war was winding down, but the Americans and English still flew missions to Germany. I heard a fighter plane overhead; it was an English plane. To my horror it exploded before my eyes. The pilot bailed out and landed a few yards from me. I rushed over to him." She paused.

Marvela gasped. "It was Robert?"

"You guessed it. He broke his foot when he landed—the other one." She twisted her mouth. "I ran to him and he said with a chuckle, 'If it takes a broken foot to meet you, I'm willing to make the sacrifice.' Do you see why I loved that man?"

Marvela nodded, "You both had such courage, and talk about a sense of humor. What happened next?"

"He leaned on me, and we made our faltering way to the hospital."

"You were definitely meant for each other," Marvela commented wryly.

"That we were. The war ended a month later. I had enough points to be mustered out, so I went back to England to wait for Robert. We were married there, attended by his family."

"So when did you come to the States?"

"I was from a small town in Illinois near Chicago. After we married, we visited my parents and siblings there. My dad asked Robert to be a partner in his medical equipment business. He worked well with my dad but was interested in law, so he attended law school part-time at the University of Chicago until he got his degree."

"Do you have children?"

"Yes, my daughter and son both live in Kansas City. Robert died ten years ago. We had fifty-five wonderful years. I came here shortly after that. I was wasting away, but the doctors couldn't find a medical reason."

"But you knew the reason," Marvela said sympathetically.

"I didn't want to live without Robert," Della replied, shaking her head.

"But you look so well now. May I ask what brought you out of it?"

"Time and my grandchildren." Della smiled. "I have six, all of them my daughter's children. Ellie was trying to homeschool them. One day she came to visit me and confessed she was totally exhausted. Her husband was too involved with his work to help her. She didn't want to give up homeschooling but felt there was no choice. She got my attention. I realized how self-absorbed I had been, and told her I would come help her. I moved in with her and helped teach the children for six years. There's no time for self-pity when you're surrounded by active children. I thoroughly enjoyed those teaching years. The children were a joy."

"So you've been back here about two years?"

"Would you believe I broke my foot," Della grimaced. "Actually, bone density tests revealed I have severe osteoporosis. At eighty-two, it was time for me to take it easier. Also the trainer, who comes three days a week, is excellent, and *Forest Glen* has state-of-the-art fitness equipment."

"I agree. I try to workout on the treadmill, but I'm not as consistent as I should be," Marvela said disparagingly. "I'll bet you're really disciplined," she added.

Della grinned. "Well, the doctor put the fear of God in me, 'Do weight-bearing exercises regularly or face a broken hip.'"

"I often wonder if the people we see using walkers and wheelchairs tried regular exercise." Marvela eyed the row of walkers.

"I sort of doubt it," Debra replied. "The trainer tells me he has a lot of trouble getting people motivated to stay on an exercise regimen."

"You've inspired me. I'm going to get on that treadmill more often," Marvela said with determination.

Della and Marvela found it easy to talk with each other. They seemed to have similar values and shared a positive outlook on life. Both of them ordered tiramisu for dessert "I bet we have more than dessert tastes in common," Marvela said as she eyed the rich dessert. "You are a delight to talk to. Thanks for sharing your amazing romance. Do you mind if I share your story with my friend Stan?"

"Of course, you can relate my story to Stan. I've seen him around and would like very much to meet him. I hope we can all get together soon," Della replied as she dipped her spoon in the dessert. "So yummy."

CHAPTER ELEVEN

Marvela was absorbed in writing poetry one afternoon when there was a knock on her door. It was the nurse who had first taken care of Flora. Marvela invited him to come in and have a seat.

"I only have a few minutes, but I have a patient who has asked for your help. He has read the newsletters you put out and has the impression that you are bigger than life." The nurse chuckled.

"Oh, the power of the media," Marvela laughed.

"Seriously, my patient Serge Kamikoff, is dying of leukemia. He speaks little English, but we're fortunate to have a nurse's aide, an émigré, who speaks fluent Russian. She has shown Serge your newsletters. He reads English better than he speaks it, and the aide helps him with words he doesn't know."

"How interesting, but how can I help him?" Marvela asked.

"He wants to talk to someone about a personal matter. He doesn't have friends or family here. He came to *Forest Glen* about five months ago—quite randomly. When he talked to the marketing director, his one requirement was that a Russian interpreter be available. He seemed quite healthy at the time, but evidently he knew he had cancer."

"Well, I'll be happy to talk with him, but it all seems a little weird," Marvela commented.

"Yes, it does, but I promised him I would talk with you. He's in hospice care now, and I don't think he has many days left."

Marvela looked at her calendar. "I could drop by tomorrow morning about ten. Would that work?"

"That should be no problem. Thank you so much. He is in room 112 in the nursing center."

Marvela hesitantly entered room 112 the next morning. Serge had his eyes closed, so she had a chance to get a good look at him. He was younger than she had anticipated; his hair was dark brown with a little gray at the temples. Although his forehead was lined, the rest of his face looked fairly smooth, but very wan. She judged him to be in his early or middle sixties.

When Zhanna, the aide, entered, she greeted Marvela in accented English and went to Serge's bedside, where she told him in Russian that his visitor was here.

He opened his eyes, tried to smile, and lifted a hand in greeting. "Velcome."

He spoke haltingly in Russian. While the aide interpreted, his eyes didn't leave Marvela's face.

"He says, thank you for coming. He feels he can trust you. He has a deep need to make a confession and a request before he dies," Zhanna paused and frowned, "which could be very soon, he says."

Marvela looked concerned as she spoke to Zhanna, "Tell him I am not clergy, or even a counselor—just a layperson. Is he aware of that?"

As Zhanna interpreted, Serge nodded his head, his brown eyes fixed on Marvela.

"He says, that is just fine; he doesn't know a clergyman or a counselor in this country. He was raised Russian Orthodox, but he has no religion now." Zhanna waited for him to continue speaking. "He has an urgent request, and he has chosen you to hear it, if you would be willing to listen."

Marvela met Serge's gaze and felt a strange kinship. "Tell him I will listen. I think he knows that whatever he tells me will be kept strictly confidential."

Tears ran down Serge's cheek as Zhanna interpreted. He reached for Marvela's hand. He kept his eyes on her as he spoke, and Zhanna interpreted.

"I came to America a year ago. I am a nuclear scientist and was one of the people responsible for Russia's nuclear energy program. I was given clearance to come to the United States to a conference on nuclear energy. I didn't go back. I was deeply disturbed by the knowledge that Russia was selling nuclear secrets to possible terrorist countries. I no longer wanted to be a part of that. Also, I knew I had leukemia, so I needed a place to go where I would be taken care of." He smiled at Zhanna. "She has made sure of that."

Zhanna blushed and kept interpreting. "There is more. I have a daughter in Russia. I have not contacted her. I know Russian authorities are looking for me."

He broke into heaving sobs. Zhanna asked him if she should call the nurse. He shook his head and gained control.

He continued speaking in a hoarse voice, and Zhanna interpreted, "He says that he wants to ask you to contact his dear daughter after he dies. He will give me the address. His daughter has a PhD in English, so she will be able to read your letter. He has some keepsakes, as well as a little money he wants her to have. He will give me the information you will need to write the letter."

Marvela nodded and addressed Zhanna, "I will do as he asked, but why me instead of you?"

"I am not yet a US citizen. He is afraid I could get into trouble," Zhanna replied. Marvela squeezed Serge's hand and kept her eyes compassionately on his as she said to Zhanna, "Tell him I understand his concern. I, too, have a beloved daughter. I will honor his request." She kissed him on the forehead.

"He says may the gods repay you."

Marvela was shaken as she left the room. She remembered her mother saying after she was diagnosed with polio. *There will be a silver lining for you somewhere, my dearest child. God's ways are mysterious.* Her experiences at *Forest Glen* indeed seemed mysteriously challenging.

As if to prove this observation, Marvela received a call from Bubbles the following day.

"I want you to know I'm in the health care center. I had a small heart attack and was hospitalized for a few days, but I'm doing fine now. I expect to be back in my apartment very soon." Her voice was weak but she sounded upbeat.

Marvela went to see her the next day. She found Bubbles sitting up in bed dressed in a ruffled pink silk bed jacket, talking on the phone. She motioned for Marvela to have a seat. After Bubbles hung up, she extended her hand. "Thanks for coming, Marvela. It's great to see you again."

Marvela clasped her hand. "Bubbles, you're looking good. I love that bed jacket."

Bubbles chuckled, "Would you believe this is the second time I've worn it in years? My daughter sent it to me, along with three other fancy numbers I've never worn when I had my appendix surgery fifteen years ago. She was a compulsive shopper."

Marvela wondered about the term *was*. "So you have family?"

A sad look passed over Bubbles's face. "My daughter died of ovarian cancer three years ago, and my oldest son was—was killed in a drowning accident as a teenager. Thank goodness for my son Kenneth, although I don't see him very often."

Marvela took Bubbles's hand. "You certainly haven't been immune from tragedy."

"This sounds like a soap opera, Marvela, but you might as well know the whole tragic story." Bubbles went on, her voice wavering. "My second husband disappeared ten years ago." Marvela was taken aback by this information, wondering how to proceed.

"Bubbles, I will certainly understand if you don't want to talk about any of this, but I'm a good listener if you want to share anything."

"I'll admit most of it is too painful to dredge up. I will say that I haven't entirely given up trying to locate my husband. I've hired detectives, but it seems to be the proverbial cold case. We have no information, or even leads. But enough of that." Bubbles wiped her eyes and said brightly, "Tell me about your life."

Although Marvela would have liked to pursue the story of the missing husband, it was obvious Bubbles wanted to change the subject. So she told Bubbles about Marie's upcoming wedding.

"Oh, a wedding in England," Bubbles clapped her hands. "My daughter got married in Italy. It was such a beautiful wedding, I shall never forget it." They talked about weddings for a while, a topic Bubbles seemed to enjoy.

Just before she left, Marvela hesitated, then asked, "Bubbles, I've had some luck locating people on computer searches—the technology is improving daily."

Bubbles's face clouded over. There was a long pause before she offered, "His name is Alexander Rogalsky."

Marvela pressed Bubbles's hand. "I'll give it my best try."

She decided to use the paid search avenue again. She came up with an Ivan Rogalsky, but not Alexander.

She tried to get in touch with Ivan Rogalsky. He lived in Chicago, so she consulted the phone directory. After trying several Rogolskys, she connected with an Ivan. She introduced herself and told him she was trying to locate Alexander Rogalsky.

There was a long pause. "Tell me why you want to know," Ivan asked, suspicion in his voice.

"I'm conducting a search for a friend who is the wife of Alexander Rogalsky."

"Could you possibly mean Bubbles?" Ivan inquired in an amazed voice.

"Well yes, but how do you know her?" Marvela asked, overcome with curiosity.

"OK, well . . . here's some of the background," Ivan replied reluctantly. "Alexander is my father, and Bubbles is my stepmother, but I've never seen her. She may not even know of my existence. I don't know where my dad is, but I have a hunch he may have changed his name and gone back to Russia. A detective interviewed me about a year ago, but I think he's lost interest in the case. Are you a detective perchance?" He asked curtly.

"No, just a friend of Bubbles. Is there a remote chance you'd like to get in touch with her?" Marvela crossed her fingers.

"Not sure. Get back with me later." Ivan hung up.

The plot thickens, Marvela thought. Did she really want to get involved? She decided to seek Stan's advice. He was acquainted with Bubbles and had spoken about his admiration for her.

That night at dinner Marvela revealed Bubbles's secrets to Stan. Stan listened attentively. "What an amazing story, and what an amazing woman. I'd never have guessed her bubbly nature hid such heartbreak."

"Nor I." Marvela buttered a roll. "Do you think I should pursue the mystery?"

Stan thought a moment. "I'll be your partner, if you like. It's too intriguing to drop, and I really would like to help Bubbles. What should we do next?"

"Don't you think I should tell Bubbles about Ivan?"

"Yes, I do. Would you like me to go with you when you break the news?"

Marvela thought it over. "Maybe I should call her and tell her I have some leads, then ask her if it would be all right to involve you."

Stan agreed this would be a wise procedure. "I'll be waiting for your call."

Marvela called Bubbles that evening. "I'll come see you in the morning and tell you about what I've discovered. Would you mind if Stan Hart got involved? He's willing to help."

Bubbles replied without hesitation, "I really like Stan, I trust him."

Stan agreed to visit Bubbles with Marvela at ten the next morning. "I think it would be best if *you* told Bubbles about your conversation with Ivan. I'll be there for backup."

Bubbles's face crumpled when she heard about Ivan. Her voice was hoarse. "I always felt Alex was hiding something from me. I knew he'd been married before. He told me that much but didn't reveal any more. We were married three years after Johnny died. Some mutual friends in St. Louis introduced us. He was an immigrant from Russia, very handsome, ten years younger than me. My friends were wary about our marriage, but I was lonely, and Alex was wonderful company." She paused and wiped a tear. "Everyone thought he married me for my money, but he seemed to be independently wealthy. There was a lot I didn't know about him."

Stan wheeled to her bedside and took her hand. "Would you like to get in touch with Ivan?" he asked gently.

"Oh yes, he could be of great help," Bubbles replied, then looked at Marvela, "don't you think?"

Marvela nodded. "But I would like to talk to him at some length before asking him to contact you."

Stan added, "I would also suggest that we do a background check on him. At this point he's an unknown factor."

Bubbles closed her eyes, suddenly exhausted. "You two do what is best. I am more than grateful for your help."

Marvela and Stan enjoyed playing detectives. Since he had an unusual name, they were able to track down quite a bit of information about Ivan. From all indications he was a law-abiding citizen. There were no records of arrests or court appearances. Satisfied, Marvela contacted Ivan again. She told him about Bubbles's condition and urged him to get in touch with her if at all possible, for Bubbles would like to see him, or at least talk to him on the telephone.

"There's really no reason I could not see her," Ivan replied after a long pause. "My mother wouldn't have approved, but she died a year ago," Ivan hesitated before going on. "I'll be coming to Kansas City on business in two weeks. If she still wants to see me, I'll look her up then." His tone was cautiously friendly.

Marvela gave him Bubbles's address and phone number. "She'll likely be back in her apartment by then. I think your visit would mean a lot to her."

True to his word, Ivan visited Bubbles, who was back in her apartment.

She called Marvela after he left.

"I can't thank you and Stan enough for getting in touch with Ivan. He's a dear boy—well man really, probably in his late forties, maybe early fifties. He looks a lot like Alex, only taller. Her voice broke, and she paused to wipe tears. "He was very close to his mother, Sophia, also a Russian immigrant. He said that Alex got in touch with him only once after we married. He, he . . ." She was sobbing.

"Bubbles, I'll come right over so we can talk in private," Marvela said. "That is, if you want me to."

"Oh yes, I need to talk to somebody," Bubbles said hoarsely.

Bubbles was sitting on the couch when Marvela arrived. Her eyes were red, but her voice was controlled as she told Marvela what she had learned from Ivan.

"Alex married me before he was divorced from Sophia. They had been separated since Ivan was a toddler, but never divorced. She got an emergency divorce when she heard about our . . . marriage." She mimed quotation marks, and her eyes filled with tears.

Marvela hugged her. "Oh, my dear, what a heartbreaking revelation! Do you know how Sophia found out about it?"

"Alex contacted Ivan about a year before he disappeared. Alex asked Ivan, a lawyer, to arrange a divorce from Sophia. He told him he was living with me as a married man. Ivan was furious and threatened to have Alex arrested for bigamy." Bubbles continued in a strained voice, "After much pleading, Ivan agreed to arrange a divorce, but on his terms. He insisted that Alex give Sophia a large monetary settlement, and stay out of their lives." Bubbles broke down in tears.

"Incredible," Marvela said, gripping Bubbles's hand. "And did you live with Alex after his visit to Ivan?"

Bubbles nodded, wiping her eyes. "Of course, I knew nothing about his marriage to Sophia, or his son. We had an amazingly happy ten months or so before Alex disappeared. I picked up that he was having some financial problems, but he didn't reveal anything about his past to me, nor did I ask. He was always very kind to me, attentive and loving." Bubbles started to tremble.

Marvela covered her with an afghan. "Do you have some medicine that might help you?"

"There are pills on my bedside table. I'll take one later. I need some time to process all of this," Bubbles said with resignation. "I'll call you when I'm feeling better." She forced a smile.

Marvela told Stan of the latest developments at dinner that evening. Stan was dismayed. "Well, there's no need to continue looking for Alex, is there? I suppose Sophia never got any money?"

"I doubt it. What a con man, but charming, it seems." Marvela shook her head.

"We do need to be as supportive to Bubbles as possible," Stan said with concern.

Marvela nodded. "After she has had some time to grieve, it might be a good distraction for us to plan a fun show," Marvela suggested.

"I'll be your number one fan," Stan said, and he kissed her hand.

Marvela and Stan looked in on Bubbles every day for a week. There were times she wanted to talk, and other times she simply appreciated their presence.

One day she greeted them cheerily. She had a new hairdo and was dressed becomingly.

"Enough of this self-pity; Alex is history. His son has turned out to be a blessing. Ivan called me last night. We had a long, friendly talk. He'll come see me the next time he is in Kansas City. As they say, this is the first day of the rest of my life."

Marvela hugged her. "What good news!"

Stan took her hand. "Bubbles, I'm so pleased."

"I've got the teapot on." She motioned them to sit at the table. "I even baked some cookies."

"What a treat," Stan said, "your cheerfulness, as well as the cookies." He chuckled.

"You look like your old beautiful self," Marvela added. "Are you ready to plan the show we talked about?"

"You bet," Bubbles replied, smiling broadly.

After several planning sessions with Kyle, they decided to have a twenties cabaret theme. Kyle would book a local over fifty-five singing group, who sang music from the roaring twenties. Their accompanist was an accomplished ragtime piano player. Bubbles would dress in her Follies costume and do the Charleston. Marvela would emcee the show, as well as put together a backdrop of pictures depicting the times. They got a local bank to provide champagne. Kyle said his budget would allow crackers and cheese.

The show was a great success. They played to an overflowing crowd. Stan surmised nearly all of the Independent Living residents were there, as well as a number of people from the assisted living units. Some relatives and friends were also in attendance.

Bubbles was ecstatic. "I haven't had so much fun since . . . well . . . since the Follies," she said to Jeanne and Leonard, who had come up to compliment her.

"And I haven't seen so much joy on the faces of the residents in a long time," Leonard commented as he hugged Bubbles.

At dinner that evening Bubbles sat with Marvela and Stan. They were so involved with accepting the accolades of residents who stopped by their table; they hardly had time to eat.

"You two did a marvelous job. I hope this will be the first of many such events." Stan reached over and squeezed their hands.

CHAPTER TWELVE

It was time for Marvela to start packing for her trip to England. She would have to shop for the right dress for the wedding, although she would buy her hat in London. She asked Bubbles to go shopping with her. They had a great time and found the right dress—a knee-length turquoise silk sheath dress with a lined lace jacket.

"Bubbles, the men in my life like to see me in this color," Marvela laughed. "But I'll have to go on a diet to look right in that slim sheath. It fits like a glove, and I don't want any bulges."

"A little extra time on the treadmill should do it," Bubbles responded. "The knee-length is a good choice, you have wonderful legs."

"The last body part to go," Marvela laughed. "You have quite a pair of gams yourself."

That evening she called Marie and told her about the dress.

"A great choice, Mom. I've chosen rainbow pastels for my wedding colors. You'll fit in beautifully. I can't wait to see it, and you."

Marvela and John had a pleasant flight to London. There was a long delay at LaGuardia, which Marvela used to call Sid, so she didn't mind.

"How's she doing?" John inquired when she returned.

"Great, she's actually been dating, and she implied he might be Mr. Right," Marvela related.

"As they say, better late than never." John laughed. "She's a great gal and deserves to be happy."

"I thought once that you might be interested in her," Marvela teased.

"Not my type," John retorted, then said seriously. "You're more to my liking."

Just then they were called to board the plane, so Marvela was spared a response. Marie and Nigel met their plane in London.

"I can't begin to tell you what a joy it is to see you two," Marie exclaimed as she hugged and kissed them. "Nigel, my parents. Don't they look great?"

Nigel greeted them warmly. He was shorter than Marvela expected, barely taller than Marie's five foot six, not handsome in the classical sense, but he had an effervescent personality that put them at ease at once.

"My parents insist you stay with them. They're rattling around in a house much too large for them, so you should be comfortable." Nigel picked up Marvela's suitcase and led them to his car.

"Nigel's mother and sisters will give you a list of things you can do to help. They're frightfully organized." Marie took her mother's arm and whispered, "I'm so glad you came with Dad."

Nigel's parents, Iris and Charles Cramer, who lived on a sprawling acreage just outside of London, greeted John and Marvela with enthusiasm.

"We're delighted you will be staying with us," Iris exclaimed as she led Marvela and John to their rooms. "We have a rather grumpy housekeeper, but she'll see to any needs you might have," Iris said as she showed Marvela her room. "Charles, be sure that John is taken care of."

"We've been married nearly fifty years, and she's never stopped giving me orders," Charles chuckled as he showed John to his room.

Marvela loved the Tudor-style house and was eager to find out more about Iris and Charles. They were probably in their early seventies, maybe late sixties. They seemed very active. Marie said they were avid horse people and would want her to ride with them.

Marvela had ridden as a teenager but had not been on a horse since. She was willing to give it a try if the horse was gentle. John had not lost the horsemanship skills he developed as a young man on the farm.

The two weeks leading to the wedding passed rapidly. The wedding reception was to be held in a large tent on the Cramer estate. "The hired help will handle all of the heavy work," Iris said, "but we could use advice on decorating. Marie tells me you have excellent taste, Marvela."

Expense didn't seem to be a factor, so Marvela suggested some exotic flower arrangements. She remembered Jane's rainbow creations with the glittering cupids, so she adopted the idea for this occasion. John suggested the guests enter through a flower-covered archway, which he would design. Iris and Charles were delighted.

The four of them went on early-morning horseback rides; a gentle horse was found for Marvela.

"Old Nell isn't quite on her last legs, but you can be sure she won't throw you," Charles told Marvela as he helped her mount.

John stayed behind with her, while Iris and Charles rode ahead on their handsome steeds.

"Aren't they a good-looking pair?" Marvela said as she began to relax on her horse.

"Never saw better-looking horses," John responded.

"Silly, I meant the humans." Marvela laughed. She was enjoying the ride.

The following day Marie took her mother shopping for a hat. After hours of looking, they found a finely woven straw creation that matched the turquoise outfit perfectly. It was an off-the-face picture brim hat. "I hope I won't impede anybody's vision," Marvela worried.

"It's picture-perfect," Marie exclaimed, "and you're a vision of loveliness."

The wedding was held in the beautiful historic Chelsea Old Church on the river Thames. Nigel's family had attended the church for generations. It was a lovely May day, with the sun flirtatiously peeking from behind clouds. The two sets of parents and Marie arrived in one limo, the bridesmaids in another, and John and the groomsmen in a third. About two hundred people were seated by Ron and Steve and two other ushers. A hundred guests had been invited to the reception.

The six bridesmaids, Nigel's three sisters and three of Marie's friends, were lovely in gowns of pink, yellow, and pale blue. The groomsmen and groom wore gray cutaways. John, who gave away the bride, chose to wear a gray tuxedo. Marie was radiant in a white satin gown with an Elizabethan collar and leg of mutton sleeves. She had chosen a trailing veil held in place by a wreath of orange blossoms.

She confided to her mother, "I was definitely influenced by the old queen." Marvela held a handkerchief to her eyes, willing herself not to cry when Marie entered on her father's arm. When John took his seat next to Marvela, he looked at her admiringly and whispered. "You look great. Thanks for choosing that color."

The ceremony was solemn and impressive. A little too much pomp and circumstance for Marvela's tastes, but this was England. The reception was another story. A string quartet played classical numbers when the guests entered. More instruments were added, and the group switched to semiclassical love songs while the guests ate. A swing band took over to play for dancing. The wooden dance floor was crowded for the slow numbers.

"Shall we join the less than nimble footed?" John chuckled as he drew Marvela to him. "Since there's hardly room to move, I think we might try it," Marvela responded. "I'm wearing medium-heeled pumps, so I shouldn't fall." Marvela laughed.

"Both of us left our canes at home, so maybe we can hold each other up," John chuckled.

It felt good to be in John's arms. Careful, an inner voice warned. When the music became lively, they took their seats. Marie and Nigel were on the floor, doing an old-fashioned jitterbug. Marie had discarded her veil and was holding up her gown with one hand. They were good, and the dance floor was cleared to give them room. The spectators clapped and cheered.

After that dance, Marie and Nigel left to change clothes. They were going on a Mediterranean cruise for their honeymoon.

Most of the guests had left by the time they returned. When they came to say good-bye to their families, Marvela gasped as she saw Marie. She was gorgeous in a turquoise silk pantsuit. She came over to kiss her father's forehead.

"Dad, you aren't the only one who likes this color." She looked at Nigel, who nodded approvingly. She hugged Marvela. "Mom, I really chose this color as a tribute to you—you're the best, you know."

Marvela kissed her daughter's cheek. "No, you're the best . . ." She let the tears flow. "Oh heck, let the mascara run. These are tears of great joy. You've made me so happy!"

That evening John and Marvela had dinner with their sons. Ron had to return to the States the following day, but Steve and his family were staying over for several days of sightseeing. The Cramers insisted they stay with them.

John and Marvela joined Steve's family for a city tour of London the next day. During the next few days they visited the popular tourist sites in London. They watched the changing of the foot guard at Buckingham Palace and the changing of the Household Cavalry at St. James's Palace. The children enjoyed the colorful spectacles.

"Grandma, I want to be a horseman when I grow up," Andrew exclaimed, "but we don't have royalty in America, do we?"

"No, Andrew," Marvela smiled, "but you can learn to ride a horse. In fact, maybe the Cramers would let you ride the gentle horse I rode. We'll check when we get back."

Andrew jumped up and down with excitement. "Oh, that would be splendid!"

John chuckled, "He's heard that word a lot these last few days. He took Marvela's hand.

"I think it would be splendid if just you and I went out to dinner tonight."

"A splendid idea," Marvela replied, squeezing his hand.

The Cramers recommended a place off the beaten track that had delicious food and a romantic ambience.

"I think it will suit you," Charles told John with a wink.

John whistled when Marvela came down the stairs. She looked chic and lovely in a black silk suit accessorized with a turquoise chiffon scarf.

He took her arm and led her to the waiting taxi. "You look great, very queenly, and I'm at your service." He kissed her hand.

At dinner, they conversed about sites in London and discussed English literature, not even mentioning their children. While sipping apricot brandy after the delicious dinner, John remarked, "We have so much in common, we should be thinking about spending a lot more time together. Have you ever thought about marrying again?"

Marvela smiled. "I'd be less than honest if I denied ever allowing such thoughts to cross my mind, but I would have to give the idea a lot of serious contemplation before I would know what is right for me."

John took her hand, "Would you contemplate seriously? I'd like so much to spend the rest of my life with you."

Marvela searched his face. "Have you completely forgiven me for my role in the custody hearings?"

"It took awhile," John admitted, "but there's no bitterness in my heart—only love." He reached over and kissed her.

Marvela's eyes filled with tears, "John, call this instant serious contemplation, but I would like to spend the rest of my life with you," she said impulsively.

They spent the night together. Before they drifted to sleep, John asked, "Any doubts, my love?"

"None, my darling. I think we're pretty amazing for two old people," Marvela replied as she covered his face with kisses.

John laughed. "You told me that age is just a number. And at your age, you're quite a number."

When they came down for breakfast, holding hands, faces glowing, Charles and Iris glanced at each other and grinned.

"The romantic ambience of the restaurant did wonders, didn't it?" Charles chuckled.

John put his arm around Marvela. "It did," he laughed. "May you be the first to know that we plan to be married—again—that is, to each other," he stammered, pulling Marvela to him.

Steve, Sonia, and the children, who had just finished eating breakfast, clapped. Steve got up and hugged his father. "This is great news."

Susan looked puzzled. "Will you still be my grandma and grandpa?" Everyone laughed.

"We'll always be your grandma and grandpa, dearest one, but we'll also be husband and wife," Marvela explained as she hugged her granddaughter.

Andrew displayed his worldly wisdom. "They will be mister and missus, and grandma won't even have to change her name."

Marvela kissed his cheek. "You've got it right, Andrew."

Iris filled all of their glasses with orange juice. "I think we should drink a toast to that."

Steve stood up and lifted his glass. "To my wonderful parents, Mr. and Mrs. Higglesford."

Andrew followed. "To my wonderful grandparents, Mr. and Mrs. Higglesford." After the congratulatory toasts, Charles said, "How about a riding excursion for the men? I believe young Andrew was promised a ride on old Nellie."

"And I have arranged a shopping expedition for the women," Iris said. Since you ladies like antiques, I thought we should visit some shops in the area. We should all have a wonderful day."

At dinner that evening, there was much to share.

"Young Andrew is going to become a splendid horseman," Charles remarked while Andrew beamed. "Ladies, tell us about your shopping expedition, did you find some treasures?" Charles asked affably.

"Oh, we did," Marvela exclaimed. "John and I were waiting to buy just the right gift for Marie and Nigel. Marie has a sugar and creamer in a china pattern she loves, but she hasn't been able to find the rest of the set. I believe I found it, but I want John to see it before we purchase it, if it's OK with John . . . John . . . John . . . ," Marvela screamed.

John's head had fallen onto the table, and he was slipping out of his chair. Steve rushed over to prop him up. "He's fainted."

The children started crying. Sonia led them out of the room.

Charles and Steve placed John's arms around their shoulders and half-carried him to a couch in the living room.

Iris ran for an ice pack. Marvela knelt by John's side and chafed his hands.

"John, can you hear me?" she pleaded. He groaned and started to open his eyes.

"Marvela, my love . . ." his head rolled to one side, and his eyes closed.

"I'll call for an ambulance, I think this is serious," Charles exclaimed as he pulled out his cell phone.

Marvela rode with John in the ambulance. She held his hand and prayed while the medics hooked up an IV. He was rushed to the emergency room, where the doctors determined he had a massive stroke. An MRI revealed he suffered a hemorrhagic stroke caused by a ruptured brain aneurysm. The doctors gave little hope for his recovery but would do surgery to try to stop bleeding in the brain if the family insisted.

"What is your prognosis if the surgery would contain the bleeding?" Steve asked the doctor.

"From all indications he would have serious brain damage even if the surgery was successful, and it may not be," the doctor said gravely.

Steve and Marvela conferred. "John once told me, he didn't want any heroic measures to save his life," Marvela said in a tear-choked voice. "I know he has a living will on file."

"I can't imagine Dad in a vegetative state," Steve said, "but I think we should get Marie and Ron's opinion before we make a decision regarding the surgery. I'll call Ron."

"And I'll call Marie. She gave me information on how she and Nigel could be contacted," Marvela said as she struggled to contain her emotions. "I really hate to disrupt her honeymoon, but she would be furious if I didn't."

Ron was not in favor of surgery. Marie was ambivalent.

"Nigel and I will be in London by tomorrow afternoon. I want to see Dad before I give my answer," Marie said through her tears.

Marvela sat by John's bedside all night, holding his limp hand.

"If only you could give me some sign, my love," she said as she kissed his cheek. "Oh God, help us make the right decision," she sobbed.

Steve and Sonia came by in the morning and urged Marvela to get some food and rest while they stayed with John.

Marvela went to the cafeteria for a cup of coffee. She tried to eat some toast, but only took several bites. She had been offered a room where she could rest, but decided to go back to John's side. When she got there the doctor was examining John.

"His vital signs are weakening. Surgery would be futile. I'm so sorry." The doctor clasped Marvela's hand before he left the room.

Marvela collapsed into a chair. "Why, oh why?" she grieved. Steve put his arms around her.

She looked at John, so pale and lifeless; maybe at some level he knew she was there. She went to his bedside, knelt beside it and took his hand.

"You were always my true love. Please go in peace knowing that," she whispered.

A nurse came in to check on John. "I'll be just around the corner should you need me." By the time Marie and Nigel arrived, John's breathing was barely audible. Marie took his hand and said through her tears, "Dad, I love you so much."

John's eyes seemed to flutter before he took his last breath. Marie hugged her mother while they both sobbed. "Oh, Mom, such a cruel twist of fate."

That night Marvela could not sleep. She cried until she was exhausted. She remembered Sylvia's words to her at a time when they shared their deep feelings: *Self—pitying thoughts are devastating. When I learned to keep them at bay, good things began to happen in my life.* Marvela tried to keep her regret-tinged thoughts from taking over. What if she would have gone to Kansas with John and kept the family together? She had never stopped loving him, but at the time she simply wasn't able to leave New York. Both she and John had made good lives for themselves she reasoned. Their recent reunion was meant to be. As she thought of their happy days together in England, Marvela felt somewhat comforted.

John wished to be cremated, so the family decided it could be done in England. They would arrange a memorial service for him in Kansas, probably sometime in June. Marie kept John's ashes for the time being.

CHAPTER THIRTEEN

Steve and his family prepared to return to the States; Marie and Marvela accompanied them to the airport. As Steve tearfully hugged his mother he said, "I wish I had been closer to Dad, but I value the few days we had together before his stroke, and I know you do too."

"They were good, and those memories mean a lot to me," she replied in a choked voice as she clung to her eldest son.

"Please plan to spend some time with us. Your grandchildren need you." Steve kissed his mother, gathered his family who took turns hugging Marvela. They blew kisses as they boarded the plane. Marvela vowed to visit Steve and his family soon after she returned to Kansas.

Marvela stayed with Marie for several days, and kept busy helping her get settled in her new home. Marvela shared the good times she had with John after the wedding. Marie talked about times she'd spent with her dad while she was in college. They didn't try to keep back their tears. It was a bittersweet week, full of grief, but with remnants of joy as they reminisced. Marvela promised to come back for the Christmas holidays.

When Marvela returned to *Forest Glen*, she found many bouquets of flowers in her apartment, along with expressions of sympathy.

Stan called and asked if she would like to join him, Jeanne, and Leonard for dinner at a nearby restaurant where they could have a secluded booth.

"That's thoughtful of you Stan. I'm not ready to face the well-meaning folks in the dining room," Marvela said gratefully.

Over dinner she related the circumstances of John's death to her friends. Although a few tears escaped, she was able to contain her emotions fairly well.

"Thanks for sharing the tough times, Marvela," Jeanne said as she hugged her. "But we'd also like to hear about the wedding."

Marvela wiped her eyes and smiled. "It was a fairy-tale wedding." She went on to describe the event.

Marvela enlisted the help of a number of John's friends and colleagues in planning the memorial service for John. It would be held in the Danforth Chapel on the University of Kansas campus the third week in June.

Marie took a plane from London; Nigel wasn't able to come. Ron and Steve flew in for an overnight; Sonia stayed at home with the children.

John was a longtime Unitarian, so the service was led by a Unitarian minister who had been a close friend of John's. He read some of John's favorite quotations and commented on his commitment to the good things in life.

"He truly seemed to live every day as if it was his last," the minister concluded. Ron gave an eloquent eulogy, recalling his dad's devotion to his young children. One of John's former students spoke of the influence John had on his life. He had been a popular professor, truly loved by many of his students. Marie didn't trust herself to speak, so Steve read a poem she had written in honor of her father.

Marvela was pleasantly surprised at the number of people who attended the service—almost two hundred. Many she had never met, reminding her of the years John had not been a part of her life. She remembered Whittier's words, *"For of all sad words of tongue or pen, the saddest are these, 'It might have been.'"*

She dabbed at her eyes as she looked around the chapel. It was a lovely day, fairly temperate for a Kansas summer. The sun shining through the beautiful stained-glass windows reflected a prism of color on the mourners. The setting and service were inspiring. John would approve.

Marie stayed with Marvela several days. She enjoyed meeting Marvela's friends and was pleased to see how well her mother had adjusted to life at *Forest Glen*.

"Mom, I think you've made yourself indispensable around here."

Marvela hugged her. "No such thing. Take the newsletter for example. Stan, Jeanne, and Leonard put out two issues while I was gone, and Stan was able to convince an in-house artist to do a comic strip." She showed Marie the newsletter.

Felix's strip was entitled, *"Give a Hoot."* It featured two old guys sitting on a bench. Ed had a tuft of hair on top of his head, and he was wearing huge horn-rimmed glasses—quite owlish looking. Gabe was a rotund oldster with a fringe of gray hair and a cherubic face—quite angelic looking.

Gabe: Why were the old days better?
Ed: Cause we were younger than.
Gabe: Say, Ed, did you know I'm approaching the age of eighty?
Ed: From which direction?

"Really clever," Marie commented. "It should bring some chuckles to the residents."

"As they say 'laughter is the best medicine,' but having a daughter like you is the best medicine of all," Marvela said as she kissed Marie's cheek.

"Mom, you may have forgotten, but I haven't," Marie said as she poured a cup of coffee for her mother. "You have a birthday in two days. I plan to stay and celebrate with you in any way you would like before I leave."

"I haven't forgotten, even though I'd rather not remember," Marvela replied with a frown.

"We celebrated Dad's life, but he wasn't there to hear it. I want to celebrate yours while you are present." Marie touched her mother's face. "And how many times have you told me to turn my frown upside down?"

"And how many times have my words come back to haunt me?' Marie said with a half smile. "What I really would like is a quiet celebration with you."

"We could have carry in Chinese food, and be sure to add lots of your favorite Crab Rangoons. Then we could spend time leisurely looking at photo albums and reminiscing."

"I'd like that, Marie." She thought awhile, and added, "Maybe Stan could join us for dessert."

"I like what you've told me about Stan, and I'm pleased he has been such a good friend. I would like to learn to know him better." Marie hugged her mother. "I think our plans are set."

"Whatever would I do without you?"

"You've done very well, but I'm so glad we can share some of the special times." Marie kissed Marvela's cheek.

The birthday celebration proceeded as planned, until Stan arrived. He entered carrying balloons and a decorated birthday cake.

"There is champagne in my carryall," he said as he wheeled over to Marvela. He reached out to kiss her cheek. "Happy birthday, dearest friend. The years look good on you." The three had a good time. Marie was impressed with Stan. She liked his sense of humor, as well as the sensitive way he treated her mother.

As mother and daughter prepared for bed, Marie watched her mother and smiled.

"You still use the same inexpensive cold cream."

"You're right. I simply don't believe the claims of the expensive ones."

"I think you should know, I agree." Marie laughed. "Like mother, like daughter."

"I hope you won't make some of the same mistakes I've had to live with," Marvela reflected.

"Like divorcing dad?"

"I guess that's one, but admitting it would be hindsight."

"And hindsight can be twenty-twenty," Marie added.

"Now you sound like your dad. Was it awful to spend so much time away from him?"

"I prayed every night that you two would get together." Her voice trembled. "My prayers were answered, but so very briefly."

They hugged each other and cried for a while.

"Looking at the photo albums was a good reminder that I had a happy childhood," Marie said, drying her eyes.

"When your father and I looked at the photos, he said the same thing. Whatever my failings, you children turned out well. Now we'd better get some shut eye, Stan will be here to take us to the airport at sixt thirty."

"That's three hours before my plane leaves, but it's probably a good idea." Marie yawned.

Marvela kissed her as she tucked her in bed. "I'll be counting the days until Christmas."

"So will I," Marie responded sleepily. "Thanks for tucking me in, Mom. I loved it."

After Marie left, Marvela got back to her routines at *Forest Glen*. She resumed calling bingo for the assisted living residents, helped with video productions, and continued to create and publish the bimonthly newsletter. She spent some time every morning at her "meditation spot" as she called it. The beautiful flowers, the rustling leaves, and the sound of the small waterfall had a healing effect. She always returned refreshed; her mind calmed. She was gradually making peace with John's passing; grateful for their reconciliation. There was still a lingering sadness, a heaviness, which she knew time would heal. There hadn't been time after their marriage announcement to dwell on a future with John. No doubt there would have been some difficult adjustments, but their love had been rekindled, and that was a comforting memory.

Her desire, now, is to live in the present, and find the joy inherent in each day. Typically, she sought out creative challenges to occupy her mind. She wanted to interview the reclusive former opera singer for the next edition of the newsletter, so she called the number for Gina Lorenzo the receptionist had given her. Her first two tries went unanswered, but a recorded voice answered on the third try.

"This is Gina Lorenzo. Please leave your name and number. I will call you back at my discretion."

Marvela left her name, number, and a message. "I am a resident of *Forest Glen*. I publish our bimonthly newsletter; maybe you have read it. I would be honored if you would grant me an interview. I believe the residents would like to hear your story, or any part of it you would like to share. I would greatly appreciate a return call. Thank you."

Three days later she got a call from Gina. "This is Gina Lorenzo returning your call," a melodious contralto voice continued, "I don't usually respond to requests for an interview, but I have read the newsletters, and I'm impressed with your work. I have decided to break my silence, actually a self-imposed exile. When would you like to set up an appointment? I would prefer a late afternoon time."

"I could come tomorrow afternoon at four o'clock, if that would work for you," Marvela responded hardly containing her excitement.

"My, you are eager. I will try to be ready at that time."

After Marvela hung up, she clapped her hands. "This should be very interesting."

Gina answered the door dressed in red satin lounging pajamas. Her jet-black hair was pulled back in a chignon, and her face looked like a porcelain doll, very few lines. Her brown eyes were heavily made-up, and her lips a vermillion red. Marvela noted a decided limp as she was led to a red velvet chaise lounge. Gina pulled over a teacart that held a gleaming silver tea set.

"I hope you like this special blend of tea. I order my supplies from England. It was my favorite when I lived in London. Do you take cream, sugar, or lemon?"

"Lemon, please." As Gina poured the tea, Marvela looked around the room. It was a reproduction of a Victorian parlor. Two stunningly beautiful Tiffany lamps were on rosewood side tables; a sparkling crystal teardrop chandelier was hung in the middle of the room. There was an exquisite rosewood secretary desk in-laid with mother-of-pearl designs.

"As you can tell, the Victorian era has great appeal for me," Gina gestured at the furnishings as she pulled over an intricately carved chair. "I started collecting the pieces when I was in England."

"It's all exceedingly lovely. I have an appreciation for antiques, and your pieces are museum quality," Marvela said with admiration.

"They are. I've been offered a fortune, but so far I have been able to hold on to them," Gina replied, a sad note in her voice. "But I'm forgetting my hostess role. Would you like some sandwiches and scones? I have clotted cream and raspberry jam, which is also sent from England. I like the tradition of English tea in the afternoon. Even though my guests are largely imaginary, I have tea every afternoon."

"This is indeed a treat. I am honored to be your guest." Marvela smiled, hesitated, and then continued, "Would you mind telling me who some of your imaginary guests might be?"

Gina made a laughing sound, but her face remained immobile. Marvela thought, *I think I understand why she has so few lines on her face.*

"Marvela, you are easy to talk with. I may reveal things to you that I haven't shared in years," Gina replied, studying Marvela closely.

"I would consider that a real privilege," Marvela replied without flinching.

"You won't reveal anything about my imaginary guests?" Gina asked, her eyes questioning along with her voice.

"It will definitely be confidential," Marvela assured her. They didn't speak for several minutes while they sipped tea and sampled the sandwiches.

"Maria Callas is a frequent guest," Gina broke the silence, and glanced at Marvela to gauge her reaction."

"Fascinating," Marvela said, nodding.

Gina cleared her throat and continued, "I was Maria's understudy in the production of *Norma* at the Lyric Opera in Chicago in 1954, so I had the opportunity to study her as well as the script."

"Was she as temperamental as the newspapers claimed?"

"This seemed to be a fairly serene time of her life, so other than her innate diva haughtiness, we didn't see much evidence of her fiery temper. She was always gracious to me. Of course this was before she met Aristotle Onassis, or at least before I knew about him."

"And the rest is history . . ." Marvela commented, laughter in her voice.

Gina raised her eyebrows. "And quite a scandalous one. Now . . . don't laugh, but we often have imaginary conversations about her involvement with Onassis. Of course she was heartbroken when he married Jackie. And as you said, the rest is history." After a long pause, she shook her head. "But you didn't come to hear about Maria Callas."

"I find her most intriguing, but at this time I would like to hear about your career." Marvela spooned some clotted cream on a scone. "Umm, delicious."

Gina nodded as she took a sip of tea.

Marvela glanced at her notes. "According to the information I gathered from the Internet, you stayed on at the Lyric Opera in Chicago for the next ten years or so, is that right?"

"Yes, I had major roles in a number of operas there."

"Any favorites?"

"Probably *La Traviata*, though *Bohème* is close. Of course I loved all of them. My time there was magical," Gina sighed, "but unfortunately it also marked the end of my operatic career."

"I believe you were injured," Marvela commented cautiously.

"Yes I was," Gina replied, a look of deep sadness in her eyes. "I injured my spine, and broke both legs in a skiing accident while vacationing in the Swiss Alps. It took me at least two years to recover completely. As you can tell, I still walk with a limp and use a cane, sometimes a walker. There were no more operatic roles for me." She took a lace-edged handkerchief from her bodice and dabbed at her eyes.

"But you did have a successful concert career." Marvela put down her teacup, and looked at Gina questioningly.

"Yes, I was in fairly high demand for about five years—mostly in Europe. I lived in London during that time, so I became quite an Anglophile. I even had a brief, very brief, marriage to an Englishman." She shook her head. "Marriage was not for me," she said with finality.

Marvela decided this was a closed subject, so she didn't ask further questions regarding the marriage.

"May I ask what brought you to this part of the USA?"

"I had a married younger sister who lived with her husband in Kansas City. She was my only sibling, and very dear to me. Her husband left her when she was in her late forties. She was diagnosed with multiple sclerosis a few months later. I moved here to take care of her."

"How tragic!" Marvela exclaimed. "Did she have any children?"

"No, after several miscarriages, she gave up trying."

There was another long silence, which Marvela didn't break. It seemed Gina needed some time to get composed.

"I know I'm considered a recluse," Gina continued, "but after my sister died, I wanted to shut off the outside world. I lived alone for a while in my sister's house, but I needed to find a place where I didn't need to worry about maintenance, and where health care was available. Mobility was a problem; I never learned to drive, and few stores delivered." She closed her eyes.

It was obvious she was beginning to tire. Marvela went to her and took her hand.

"You have a most fascinating story to tell, and I am delighted you chose to share some of it with me. I have many more questions, but I don't want to wear out my welcome. I would like to come back another day, if you would have me. We haven't talked about how you came to be an opera singer."

Gina opened her eyes, and half smiled. "Now that I've started to tell my story, it's like the dam has been broken. I guess I'm ready to talk to someone, and you seem to be that person. I will call you in a few days."

"I'll be waiting for your call. Thank you again for your willingness to share your story with me." Marvela clasped Gina's hand in both of hers.

"It turned out to be my pleasure," Gina said softly.

Marvela smiled all of the way back to her apartment.

CHAPTER FOURTEEN

Marvela wanted to share her time with Gina, so she called her friend Sid.

Sid's machine answered, "This is Sid Langley. Please leave message. Your call is very important to me."

"Hey girl, pick up the phone, this really is an important message," Marvela said, emphasizing 'important.' "

Sid picked up the phone. "Marvela, our ESP is working, I was thinking of you."

Marvela giggled. "I wonder how many important messages you return?"

"You know me too well my friend. What's up?"

"Remember the opera singer recluse I told you about?"

"You interviewed her!" Sid exclaimed.

"What an interesting character." Marvela went on to tell Sid about the interview.

"I plan to be in KC next month, maybe she'll let me photograph her then," Sid said hopefully.

"She may, or may not, but I'll ask her," Marvela responded. "I'm excited about your upcoming visit. You will stay with me."

"Of course. You can help me plan my wedding."

"You're kidding!" Marvela exclaimed.

"Nope, marriage is definitely in the picture, but we'll probably go to a justice of the peace. I plan to strike while the iron, make that man, is hot." Sid laughed.

"I hope you plan to have a decent reception," Marvela advised. "You know I'll fly to New York if I'm invited."

"Consider it done," Sid said firmly, and then added, "But I will need to consult with Tyrone. I'll tell you all about him when we can chat for hours."

"Can't you give me an advance preview?" Marvela pleaded.

"Well, he's seventy, and still works as a meteorologist. He gives weather reports on the radio now, but he has been on television," Sid answered with pride in her voice.

"So he is handsome and has a voice to die for?"

"I think so. He's balding, but has a neat mustache—the kind that tickles." She giggled. "But best of all, he's sweet and kind, and he loves me," Sid said with a smile in her voice.

"I'm so pleased. You deserve all of the happiness you can find."

That night at dinner Marvela told Stan about her conversation with Sid.

"She sounds so happy," Marvela concluded.

Stan reached over and took her hand. "I wish that kind of happiness for you. We hope the old Marvela sparkle will return soon."

"I felt some of the 'old spark' yesterday, after I interviewed the reclusive Gina Lorenzo."

Marvela shared some of the highlights of her visit to Gina.

"This place holds so many fascinating stories. I'm so pleased you are finding them," Stan said as he looked at her, admiration in his eyes.

"Your support means a lot to me, dear friend," Marvela said squeezing his hand.

Marvela was just completing the first September edition of *New Horizons* when the phone rang. It was Gina inviting her to come over for another interview.

"I'd enjoy another teatime visit, if that would work for you, Marvela." Gina's voice was warm and inviting. "Tomorrow at four would be good for me."

"I'll be there. By the way, a professional photographer friend of mine will be in town next week. Any chance you'd be willing to have your picture taken?"

There was a long silence. *I've blown it*, Marvela thought.

Finally Gina responded, "I'm not ready for that kind of exposure, dear, but I will allow you to use a photograph from my operatic days." Gina's voice was still friendly.

The next afternoon she greeted Marvela, looking regal in a royal blue hostess gown. She gave her half smile, but this time it showed in her eyes.

"It's good to see you again, Marvela. You look very attractive today. That is a good color on you."

Marvela wore a pale blue gauzy pantsuit, and had given extra care to her makeup.

Gina wheeled out the teacart. "I've been experimenting with a smoked salmon sandwich spread. I hope you like it," she said as she poured tea.

Marvela sampled one. "They're delicious; you're quite a gourmet cook."

"Not really, but I do like to try different teatime recipes," Gina replied modestly. "Please try the biscuits, specially ordered from England."

They engaged in small talk while enjoying the food. After her second cup of tea, Marvela asked Gina, "Would you mind telling me about your background, and how you became a renowned opera singer?"

Gina put down her cup, and cleared her throat. "I doubt if you read anything about my childhood in the Internet accounts. Its something I don't talk about." She blotted her lips on a monogrammed linen napkin. "Since talking to you last, I've done a lot of soul-searching. It will be difficult for me, but I'm ready to tell my story."

"And I'm ready to listen." Marvela nodded and smiled.

There was a long pause before Gina began in a soft voice, nearly a whisper. "Like Loretta Lynn, I was a coal miner's daughter. There was food on the table as long as my father worked, but he was afflicted with a lung disease, common to many miners, so he worked sporadically. My mother worked as a maid to one of the mine managers, but was fired when she was caught taking food from the pantry. She wasn't able to find steady work after that. My sister and I knew she was simply trying to feed us. In desperation, my father would work in the mines when he was very sick. Of course that took a heavy toll on his health, and he died when I was thirteen. Mother, my sister, and I lived with our grandmother, but she had little food to spare." Gina closed her eyes and didn't speak for several minutes.

"Would you like me to come back another time?" Marvela asked gently.

"No, I'd like to continue. I may not get up enough courage another time." Gina responded in a stronger voice. "My grandmother took us to a large Baptist Church, and insisted that I sing in the choir. I was grateful for robes that covered my shabby clothes. I was soon given solo parts, and I received many compliments on my singing. The mine owner's wife took an interest in me, and asked me to live with them as a nanny for their young son. In return she paid for voice lessons, and gave me a generous clothes allowance. At seventeen, I was urged to enter the Miss West Virginia contest. I was second runner up, but won the talent contest. Friends of the mine owner, who lived in New York, were impressed with my voice. The couple asked me to live with them in the city. They paid for voice lessons, and before long I auditioned for chorus roles at the Met." Gina paused and looked at Marvela as though asking for permission to continue.

Marvela smiled at her. "That was a fortuitous turn of events. So what happened next?"

"I was hired for the Metropolitan Opera chorus, and a few months later I was given small solo parts. When asked to understudy the great Callas at the Lyric Theater in Chicago, I couldn't refuse. You know the rest." Gina gave a sigh of relief, and rested her head on the back of her chair.

Marvela went to her, hesitated, and then hugged her. "It is such an honor for me to hear your story."

Gina hugged her back. "While it has been difficult to relate, I needed to talk about this time in my life. You have helped me release a burden. I consider you a friend, in need and deed."

"I will keep your story confidential, until you give me permission to share it," Marvela assured her.

"I would prefer to keep the incidents of my childhood untold, for the time being. But you may use anything else I have related."

"I would like to feature that part of your story in our newsletter, but I will show it to you before it is printed. I didn't take notes, or tape our interview, so I will need to ask you to check out pertinent facts."

"That would please me. Hopefully we can have tea again?" Gina half smiled.

"And that would please me." Marvela smiled brightly, and added impulsively. "If you would like to have dinner with me in the dining room, I would welcome your presence."

"How about tomorrow night, before I get cold feet," Gina responded without hesitating. "This will be my first visit to the dining room. When I don't cook, I order my meals over the telephone."

"We have a date, Gina," Marvela said enthusiastically. Would six o'clock be too early?"

"Yes, but I understand the dining room closes at six thirty, so I'll come to your apartment at six, and we can go together. I will need your supportive presence. By the way, do they dress for dinner?"

"No, the dress is quite casual. No jeans, of course," Marvela added, grinning. "But feel free to wear what is comfortable for you."

As Marvela anticipated, some of the residents gasped, and a few openly stared when she and Gina were led to their table. Gina looked elegant in a red linen pantsuit, her jet-black hair pulled back in a French twist. Marvela had asked for a partially hidden table in a corner of the room, so they could have as much privacy as possible.

Gina breathed a sigh of relief when she was seated. "As you know, Marvela, I have become quite agoraphobic. This is not easy for me."

Marvela took her hand. "But in my opinion it is a courageous first step. When you come again, I'd like to introduce you to one of my good friends," Marvela told her about Stan.

"He sounds like someone I would enjoy meeting. Maybe I'll return in a few days, that is if the food is good." Gina chuckled, her face almost opening into a smile.

Marvela called Stan after dinner and related Gina's progress.

"Marvela, you're a marvel," Stan laughed. "How about a celebratory dinner off the premises, and a movie tomorrow night?"

"I'd love that," Marvela replied.

As usual, Marvela had a good time with Stan. They had endless things in common, so the conversation was always lively. After dinner they opted to go to Stan's apartment and watch a DVD of Michael Moore's movie, *Sicko*.

After the movie they became engrossed in a conversation about the health care system. This led to speculation about the health care of the residents at *Forest Glen*.

"I think some of the residents in assisted living are over medicated," Marvela speculated. "Of course, I am a minimalist when it comes to medication."

"You're undoubtedly right. I've always believed that an ounce of prevention is worth a pound of prescription drugs." Stan chuckled. "Of course, I didn't refuse drugs when I was in a lot of pain," he added ruefully. "At that time morphine was a good friend."

"Painkilling drugs helped me through some rough times," Marvela admitted, "but I also try to practice relaxation and visualization techniques, which seem to be helpful. I once read that we have an internal pharmacy that could be tapped, if we just knew how to do it. The idea fascinates me, but I have so much to learn in that area."

"There are many mysteries that pure science hasn't addressed. Although the little I've read about quantum physics leads me to believe that science and mysticism aren't as unrelated as we may have thought," Stan commented thoughtfully.

"What do you think about having a column in the newsletter that addresses some of these issues?" Marvela queried.

Stan responded enthusiastically, "I think it's an excellent idea. How about using a question and answer format? Of course we may have to pose the first few questions."

"Sounds workable," Marvela agreed. "I'm sure we could call on some experts in the field to help us answer questions. Especially the queries that may be too tough to glean from the available literature," Marvela said wrinkling her forehead.

"If you approve, I'll volunteer to coordinate the column. It's an area I would like to explore," Stan offered.

Marvela took his hand. "Stan, that would be great. This has been quite a productive evening."

"And most enjoyable," Stan said as he kissed her hand.

The next day Sid called from a downtown bookstore. "Any chance I could stay with you this weekend? This is the fifth city on my book signing tour, and I'm really getting weary."

"How exciting, Sid. Please come here for an R and R. We can stay in bed all day, or do whatever you want. I'll be at your command."

"A day in bed sounds wonderful. But we might cook up a stimulating diversion for the next day," Sid responded with her infectious giggle.

Sid is like a refreshing drink on a hot day, Marvela thought. *I wonder what we could do that would be different and fun. She'll probably have some good ideas.*

"The bed is waiting for you," Marvela told Sid when she arrived late that night.

"I really am exhausted, and just a little tipsy," Sid admitted. "The bookstore owners had a dinner in my honor, and the wine flowed too freely."

Sid slept until noon the next day. After a long shower, she found Marvela in the kitchen.

She kissed Marvela's cheek. "Nothing like the smell of frying bacon to get the juices flowing. What have you planned for the day?"

"I thought we'd spend a few hours catching up on our lives." Marvela hugged Sid. "I'm really eager to see your book, and hear how the sales are going. Of course we have to talk about Tyrone. I want a detailed account."

After enjoying a leisurely breakfast, they curled up on the couch in the living room. Sid showed Marvela her book of baby pictures.

"Your creativity astounds me, Sid. I like all of them, but the newborn nestled in an opening rose bud is poignantly exquisite. How did you do that?"

"I'll admit to some superimposing, or cutting and pasting, if you will. But the trick is to make it look like real time. A good many of my pictures are candid shots, especially older babies."

"Like this one of the one-year-old stuffing his mouth with birthday cake, chocolate frosting all over his face and hands."

"He was such fun. He kept calling out 'mine, mine" chortling all the while."

They had an animated conversation for several hours. Sid wanted to hear the particulars of Marie's wedding and John's tragic stroke and passing.

Marvela related the series of events to Sid.

"We've probably gone through a box of tissues, but there's nothing as healing as crying with a good friend," Marvela said as she wiped her eyes.

Sid took her hand, "We've been through a lot together, and I know we'll be bonded friends forever." She laughed, "Now I'm waxing poetical."

Marvela kissed her hand. "I don't know what I'd do without you. But now I want to hear all about your wedding plans. Have you set a date?"

"We'll probably go to a justice of peace when I get back. No fanfare. But my daughter insists that we have a gala reception, which she offered to plan. You'll come, won't you?" Sid queried, a pleading look in her eyes.

"I'm definitely planning on it," Marvela assured her. "It's an auspicious day for you, and it would be fun to see some old friends—and haunts—in New York after the wedding."

CHAPTER FIFTEEN

Sid and Marvela had dinner with Stan in the dining room. Much to Marvela's amazement, Gina was dining with Jane at a nearby table. She brought Sid over to introduce her to them.

After engaging in polite acknowledgments, Jane said excitedly, "Marvela, this *is* a small world. It's almost impossible to believe, but Gina and I sang in the same Baptist choir in Melville, West Virginia when we were teenagers. I had a passable singing voice, but Gina sang like an angel." She smiled broadly at Gina.

"That is amazing!" Marvela exclaimed. "How did you ever discover this?"

Gina replied, with almost a full smile. "Jane saw me in the dining room with you, and remembered me after all of those years."

"I called her and told her who I was, and asked if we could meet." Jane looked at Gina questioningly before going on. After Gina nodded, Jane continued, "Her first response was 'I'm very busy now, may I call you back?'"

"I had to have time to regroup," Gina explained. "I remembered Jane Simmons, and was both fearful and delighted about seeing her again. Her father was an official in the mining company. Jane was always kind to me, unlike some of the other girls of her status. But, as you know Marvela, I didn't think I was ready to reveal all of my past."

Jane smiled, looking a bit smug. "But she called me the following day."

"As I said, Marvela, the dam was broken, and Jane is as kind and understanding as you have been." Gina reached for Marvela's hand. "I was such a lonely prisoner of my fears, and have kept people at bay for so long. Now I'm discovering a new world of friendship, and it is quite wonderful." Tears formed in her eyes.

Marvela kissed her cheek. "Gina, finding you is like discovering a precious jewel." Marvela took Sid's hand. "Friends are priceless."

When they rejoined Stan, Sid commented, "Wow, this place is a storehouse of amazing stories."

"I sometimes wonder how many are kept secret as Gina's was." Stan reached over and took Marvela's hand. "But this lady is doing a great job of uncovering them."

Back in Marvela's apartment Sid started pacing the floor.

"OK friend, tell me about it. I remember the pacing as the first steps of a creative aha," Marvela prodded Sid.

"I'm thinking about an idea for another book. The babies represented the beginnings of life, and the beautiful faces here speak of life's ending time. I'd like to take dozens, maybe hundreds, of pictures of faces at *Forest Glen*." She wrinkled her forehead. "Could we start tomorrow?"

"My calendar is cleared, as I said you can call the shots," Marvela said with a crooked grin. "How can I help?"

"You can make some calls to see if it would be OK for us to visit and take some pictures," Sid replied as she continued pacing.

"I'll start with Gina, but keep your fingers crossed." Marvela held up her crossed fingers—on both hands.

"I'm sure one day won't cut it. If she's not ready now, she may be soon," Sid said. "Maybe I can convince Tyrone to come back with me after we're married."

"First things first," Marvela laughed. They spent the next day taking pictures. Sid kept her camera clicking, and got some fantastic pictures. She spent the rest of the day taking candid shots of *Forest Glen* residents. Gina consented to have her picture taken if Marvela and Sid would come to tea. They agreed without hesitation.

At tea that afternoon Gina greeted them wearing a flowing white hostess gown with a split skirt. A pearl studded comb in her hair held a low knot in place; a few tendrils curled around her face. She looked softer, and very lovely.

"Real friends are so much better than imaginary ones," Gina said as she winked at Marvela.

Sid printed the photos she had taken of the residents on the computer, and showed them to Marvela. There was an attractive elderly couple holding hands as they walked down the hallway, a woman in a wheelchair shelving library books, a wizened gray-haired woman at the computer, six seventy-to-ninety-year-old women kicking their heels in the swimming pool, five laughing men around the breakfast table—canes and walkers in sight, a husband serving breakfast to his wife in a wheelchair, the "Happy Hookers" knitting group admiring each other's work; a group of laughing women—mostly octogenarians, playing bridge; residents taking turns competing at virtual bowling on a Nintendo Wii video game console; an eighty-nine-year-old woman sitting at an easel, painting in oils; an attractive ninety-plus-year-old with amazingly nimble fingers playing a grand piano, a ninety-three-year-old composer carefully transferring his musical notations to manuscript paper.

The pictures of Gina were exquisite. "What a beauty!" Sid exclaimed.

"They're all really great!" Marvela proclaimed. "You've caught a cross-section of life in *Forest Glen*. With your permission, I'd like to use some of them in the newsletter."

"I would be honored. When I come back I'd like to do some close-up portraits. There's a story in each of these faces," Sid said as she admired the pictures.

"I'm reminded of the song Stan and I heard in the Unity Church Sunday, 'You are the face of God . . . You are a part of me . . . .'"

"Have you found a church that meshes with your philosophy of life?" Sid inquired.

"Unity comes close, but this was our first visit. Stan considers himself a sacred humanist, and I see myself as spiritual, but not really religious. We've been visiting various places of worship, including a Jewish synagogue and Buddhist temple."

"You're really eclectic. As you know I'm a lapsed Catholic, but I still find some of their rituals meaningful to me," Sid said thoughtfully.

"I believe that humankind was somehow programmed to worship something greater than themselves, although religion has certainly divided us," Marvela mused.

"Believe as I do or you're toast," Sid said wryly.

"Oh, the saving grace of humor." Marvela chuckled.

Stan insisted on taking Sid to the airport, and of course Marvela rode along. As they hugged their good-byes, Sid reminded Marvela of her promise to attend the wedding.

"I want you to be an honored witness at our ceremony," Sid said as she held both of Marvela's hands. She went over to Stan and took his hand. "And I'd love to have you come, if your schedule permits."

"I'll check my calendar. It might work out," he said looking expectantly at Marvela.

"I'd like your company Stan. We'll make it work," Marvela said with a fond smile.

In the weeks before the trip to New York, Marvela found herself caught up in another *Forest Glen* mini drama.

One of the bingo players in assisted living had been a puzzle to Marvela. Rosie, at seventy-three, was probably one of the youngest residents at *Forest Glen*. Because she was cognitively and physically able, she was allowed to leave the "neighborhood" (as it was called), anytime she wanted to. Why she was housed in assisted living was a mystery to Marvela.

Rosie always helped clean up after bingo, and would talk with Marvela during that time. Sometimes she was late for bingo saying she was walking around outside. When she returned she would smell of cigarette smoke, and Marvela surmised she had been smoking. One evening after the bingo items were stashed away, and all of the chairs put in order, Rosie asked if she could talk confidentially with Marvela.

"I did a stupid thing, Marvela," she began, then hesitated.

"You're not the first," Marvela smiled encouragingly.

"You probably noticed I smoke?'

Marvela nodded.

"I purchase cigarettes when I go to town," Rosie paused to take a deep breath. "This morning I was caught going out the door without paying for a carton I had picked up." Her voice wavered. "When I told them where I lived, they let me go. They said they would report my thievery to the administration at *Forest Glen*. One of my problems is momentary forgetfulness, kind of a short blacking out. It happens very rarely." She was sobbing.

Marvela took her hand, "Has this happened before, that is, taking something from a store?"

"Never," she said emphatically. "I've had memory lapses before, but I haven't shoplifted." She hiccoughed and dried her eyes.

"So what is the worst thing that could happen?" Marvela inquired sympathetically.

"I would lose my privileges to go out on my own. I couldn't bear that." Tears ran down her cheeks. "Do you think you could help me?" She dried her eyes.

"I don't have any authority; I'm a resident like you. What do you think I could do?"

Rosie replied with dry-eyed conviction. "For one thing, I'll need a character witness, preferably someone who is not on the staff. You are so articulate, and I think you have some power—the newsletter and all. Maybe you could plead my case for me."

"Have you been called by anyone in administration yet?" Marvela inquired.

"No, I talked to one of the secretaries, a friend of mine, and she said they were all involved in a planning retreat today. So I'll probably be called tomorrow." Rosie looked at Marvela entreatingly.

Marvela sighed. "Well, if I agree to represent you." she shook her head and cleared her throat, "like a lawyer without portfolio—I'd like a little more information. For starters, why are you in assisted living when you seem so independent?"

Rosie looked pained. "Money is probably the bottom line. I need Medicaid help, and I couldn't get it if I had an apartment in Independent Living."

"Please excuse my bluntness, Rosie, but you seem able to get along in the outside world. Do you have family?"

"That's part of the problem," Rosie sighed. "I lived with my daughter, a single mom, and things seemed to be going well. She worked long hours, and I cooked and cleaned, and looked after her two teenagers when necessary." She paused.

"So what happened?" Marvela prodded gently.

"I had a petit mall seizure—the first in my life." Rosie's breathing became labored. "Unfortunately it happened when I was frying chicken." She stopped to catch her breath. "The grease caught on fire," she moaned. "Robbie, the teenage son, arrived in time to put it out."

"You said petit mall, so did you recover quickly?"

"Oh yes, I was sitting by the table, and got up when Robbie came in. I started helping him clean up, but it really scared him . . . and . . ." She lowered her head.

"And the rest of the family, I assume," Marvela filled in.

Rosie nodded. "My daughter was afraid to leave me alone. The doctor said if I took medication, I probably wouldn't have any more seizures, but my daughter wasn't convinced. She was worried that I might not take the medications regularly, so she arranged for me to live here where medication could be monitored."

"So have you had any more seizures?"

"I've lived here for two years, and haven't had one." Rosie's voice was vehement.

"And the memory lapses?" Marvela asked.

"So infrequent I could count them on one hand—and they're always very brief," Rosie replied convincingly.

Marvela thought awhile. "I'll go with you to your 'hearing,' and support your case. But there's no guarantee they'll take a chance on letting you go out on your own," Marvela told her gently but candidly.

Rosie called Marvela the next morning and asked her to accompany her to the administrative offices, where the CEO, a social worker, and nurse were present. Rosie answered questions quite calmly, relating events as she had shared them to Marvela. Marvela told how Rosie had always appeared competent and able to handle her affairs. She would like to see her get another chance. The CEO said they would confer about the case and get back with Rosie soon.

A few days later Marvela got a call from Rosie.

"I can't go out on my own anymore," her voice was choked. "I can only go out when accompanied by another adult."

"I'm so sorry," Marvela sympathized. "Do you think your daughter would go with you occasionally?"

"She might, but I'm hesitant to ask her, she's so busy," Rosie paused. "Of course I do go to her house about once a week to help out. Hopefully, I can continue that, but I really love to go to the Plaza or to the Crown Center."

"Rosie, I'll commit to taking you to the Plaza, or to a mall, at least twice a month. The dates might be erratic, but I'll let you know ahead of time."

"You're an angel, Marvela. Maybe if I prove myself with you, I'll be able to go back to taking the bus by myself."

"We'll give it a try," Marvela promised.

At dinner the following evening Marvela related Rosie's dilemma to Stan, Jeanne, and Leonard.

"Leonard and I enjoy an occasional trip around town, mostly to window-shop or try a new restaurant; we could take her with us on occasion, right honey?" Jeanne gave him a coquettish grin.

"She's a hard one to refuse." Leonard kissed her cheek. "I'd sure hate to have my independence curtailed, but this one will keep me going until I drop from fatigue."

Marvela laughed. "You two are an inspiration to me. You'd make a good comedy team. Maybe you should work up an act and visit some of the shut-ins."

"You know, that's really a good idea," Stan chimed in. "It makes more sense than some of the entertainment Kyle pays big bucks for."

Marvela added, "It might also help engender a sense of community by getting more of the nearly reclusive residents involved."

CHAPTER SIXTEEN

When Marvela got back to her apartment there was a message from Nina Phillips on her answering machine.

"Hi Marvela, this is Nina, a voice from your past. I've never forgotten how you went to bat for me when I was laid off from ABC. Would you call me back? I have a favor to ask."

Nina must be close to ninety by now. Marvela thought. *I'll call her right back.* Nina answered after the first ring.

"Nina, how good to hear from you," Marvela said warmly. "Tell me about yourself"

"I live in an assisted living center in upstate New York, close to my daughter who is an editor at the *Syracuse Post Standard.*"

"What a small world. I once was hired as a reporter there, but broke my contract when my parents were killed, and I moved to New York. Your daughter followed in your footsteps—another writer. Do you still do any writing?"

"I try to," Nina replied. I'm quite crippled from arthritis, but I can still type with two fingers." Nina laughed.

"You sound great. How can I help you?"

"I've been commissioned to write a small book on *The Secrets of Graceful Aging.* I know you are younger than I am, but I'm gathering information from people over seventy. Have you passed that mark?"

"Sure have. I live in a retirement community now. There are people here who have aged very gracefully. I could share some of the observations I've gathered from interviews with some of these remarkable people, and maybe add some of my own."

"That would be wonderful. If you give me your e-mail address, I'll send you the guidelines as well as my address and phone number."

Marvela gave her the information. "It's great to hear from you. I'm so pleased you are still writing. Your book will be an inspiration to the readers."

"I'm looking forward to your contributions, Marvela. You have been an inspiration to me. You encouraged me to keep writing. After I left ABC I published two novels, which did fairly well."

"I wish I'd known that earlier. I will certainly look them up. I'm always looking for a good read. May I ask how you found me?"

"Actually, it was a bit round about. My granddaughter, who just had a new baby, bought a wonderful book of baby pictures which she shared with me. I noted that the photographer was Sid Langly, and I remembered she was a friend of yours. So I looked her up in the New York directory. After a few wrong numbers, the right Sid answered. You've obviously been in touch with her quite recently."

"What a great memory, you have," Marvela exclaimed. "To my knowledge you only met her once at a dinner party at my house."

Nina chuckled, "Sid's hard to forget, as are you for that matter. But I am grateful for a retentive memory, although I often forget where I put my glasses." She laughed.

"I can relate to that." Marvela chuckled. "You know one of the pleasures of getting old is getting in touch with friends from our past. You've made my day."

After hanging up, Marvela went to her computer and tried to summarize what she had learned about graceful aging from people she'd met at *Forest Glen*.

Inside of every older person is a younger one waiting to express her/himself. I have interviewed a number of inspiring elders at Forest Glen Retirement Community. When I interviewed Bubbles (ninety), it didn't take long to find the young Ziegfield chorus girl, eager to tell her story. I would say her secret to aging gracefully is her positive "bubbling" attitude toward life. She told me once, she spends at least fifteen minutes before she gets up in the morning on "attitude adjustment." "Sometimes it takes longer," she admitted, "but I try not to get out of bed until I feel I'm in a positive groove."

Others who deserve mention are: Marvela (seventy-five) who does the five Tibetan exercises, called The Fountain of Youth, every day. It is a type of Yoga exercise that enhances body, mind, and spirit. Neva (eighty-one) worked part-time in administration until she was eighty. She now fills her days with volunteer work. She states she is busier than ever. Jeanne (eighty-three) taped the following poem to her bathroom mirror:

Let me grow lovely, growing old—
So many fine things to do:
Laces and ivory, and gold
And silks need not be new,

And there is healing in old trees,
Old streets a glamour hold.
Why may not I, as well as these
Grow lovely growing old.

(Anon)

Leonard (eighty-four) makes it a point to laugh out loud as often as possible. He watches tapes of Laurel and Hardy, and other comedians, to stimulate laughter on days when he's feeling low. He believes that laughter "charges youthful energy."

Creative expression is another antidote to aging gracefully. Margaret (eighty-nine) paints beautifully and often. The walls outside her apartment are a changing gallery of lovely oil paintings, a testimony to her creativity. Henry (eighty-eight) writes poetry. He has written over sixty clever rhymes in the last two years. Walter (ninety-three) is a composer. His compositions for full orchestra are performed by local high schools. Rochelle (eighty-five) is a quilter. She is creating exquisite quilt patterns to give to her eight grandchildren. Felix (eighty-eight) creates original comic strips. His clever contributions to a retirement community newsletter keep residents laughing. At Forest Glen twelve members of a writing group (ages sixty-eight to eighty-nine) submit original pieces each week. There is no critiquing; participants are thereby encouraged to write for fun and therapy.

All of these people have a zest for life that shows in their faces as well as in their creative products. One of the creators commented, "When I create, my mind feels young and vital."

Creative expression does not necessarily have to result in a product. Living creatively is part of a lifestyle that looks for new ways to do old tasks. Something as simple as brushing our teeth with the opposite hand, or finding new routes to old destinations can forge new pathways in our brain. We're told we lose millions of brain neurons as we age. Although they cannot be replaced, we can reenergize the ones we have. Marian Diamond, a brain researcher, claims we can continue to add glia cells (those that nourish the neurons) well into old age, as long as we take part in stimulating activities.

Marvela wanted to conclude the piece with some hints for a long and healthy life.

She wrote several paragraphs, but wasn't satisfied with her conclusions—too preachy. She went through her files seeking inspiration and found it.

Among yellowed clippings in my files, I found this piece by John A. Schindler that pretty much says it all:

How to Live a Hundred Years Happily

1. Do not be on the lookout for ill health.
2. Keep usefully at work.
3. Have a hobby.
4. Learn to be satisfied.
5. Keep on liking people.
6. Meet adversity valiantly.
7. Meet the little problems of life with decision.
8. Above all, maintain a good sense of humor.
9. Live and make the present hour pleasant and cheerful.
10. Keep your mind out of the past, and keep it out of the future. Remember age is just a number!

—marvela higglesford

Marvela showed her writing to Stan at dinner that night. He had just returned from his therapy sessions at NIT.

After reading the piece Stan commented, "Marvela, you epitomize the concept that creative expression is a powerful antidote to aging."

"Thanks Stan, and you epitomize the power of the will. How were your sessions at NIT?"

"The best yet," Stan enthused. "I was able to stand and take a few steps."

"Terrific! How did you accomplish that feat?"

"It was an experimental hybrid system that uses a combination of electrical stimulation and walkers," Stan explained with growing excitement. "Since my spinal cord wasn't entirely severed, and I have some residual control of the muscles in my legs, I am an ideal subject for this procedure. In the near future I will be a guinea pig for a spinal implant experiment."

"Wow, scientists are really making progress. Tell me more about the implant procedures," Marvela queried with interest.

"Well, as I understand it, movements such as walking aren't entirely controlled by the brain. Instead, once the brain has sent a signal to start walking, feedback loops between the motor nerves in the lower spinal cord, and the sensory nerves in the muscles largely control the process. So in theory, if the nerves beneath a spinal injury are undamaged (and mine seem to be OK), an implant will boost the signals from the brain and allow the reflexes to take over. More than you wanted to know?" Stan smiled as his eyes questioned.

"Oh no, it is all so fascinating!" Marvela exclaimed.

"Of course, the doctors keep telling me to temper my expectations. It will take time for the kinks to be worked out."

"The devil is in the details." Marvela chuckled.

Just before they left the dining room, Mary wheeled her way to their table. Marvela had talked to her a few times since their first dinner together, mostly greetings in passing. Mary seemed to have shrunk, and she was very pale.

"I'm sorry to bother you, Marvela. We haven't been very close, but I enjoy reading your newsletters very much. It has really helped bring a sense of community to this place. I've also heard, by the grapevine, that you have been personally helpful to many people here. I wonder if I could ask you to help me?" She asked tentatively.

"Certainly, Mary. What may I do for you?"

Mary blew her nose and wiped her eyes. "I'm dying of cancer. It's terminal. I have chosen to stay here as long as I can, under the care of hospice workers who visit me several times a week."

Marvela took Mary's hand. "I'm so sorry to hear this. Is there something special you want me to do?"

She squeezed Marvela's hand. "I've heard that you are good at finding people. This one may be very difficult—in many ways. First it will be very hard for me to tell this story." She pulled out a handkerchief and wiped her forehead. "I often get cold sweats, especially when I get upset."

"Would you like me to come to your apartment? Do you need some meds?" Marvela inquired sympathetically as she nodded to Stan, who waved and went on his way.

"That would be so good of you. The hospice nurse will be here in an hour to give me a shot. I think a cup of hot tea might do until then."

Marvela pushed the wheelchair to Mary's apartment where she got her settled on a recliner, covered her with an afghan, and brewed a cup of tea.

After taking a few sips of the hot drink, Mary seemed to calm down. "Thank you so much, Marvela, I think I can talk now."

Marvela sat on the couch facing her. "Take your time, Mary. I don't have any deadlines today."

Mary swallowed, started to talk, but couldn't go on. She covered her eyes with a handkerchief she took from her sweater pocket and sobbed. "P-please forgive me, Marvela."

Marvela put her hand on Mary's arm and repeated reassuringly, "Take your time."

Mary took a few sips of tea and seemed to gain control. "You're the first person, other than my parents, I've told this to." She wiped her eyes. Maybe I should let the secret die with me, but I just can't." After a long pause she continued, her voice wavering. "I had a baby girl when I was sixteen. My parents placed me in a home for unmarried pregnant girls outside of Chicago until the baby was born." Her body shook with sobs.

Marvela handed her a box of tissues and massaged her shoulders. After a few minutes the sobs subsided, and she continued. Her voice was so soft; Marvela had to strain to understand her. "I never saw the baby. I was told she was adopted by a good family. At that time adoption papers were sealed. I bribed one of the nurses by giving her my ruby ring—a graduation gift from my wealthy grandmother. I wanted the nurse to find out the name of the family who adopted my angel. The nurse didn't come back." She stifled a sob. "But five years later, just before my marriage, I received a letter from nurse Barbara. It seemed she wanted to clear her conscience. She told me the adoptive family's last name was Hensley. I secretly looked up the name in phone books of every city we visited. I called a few, but would hang up before I made an inquiry." She sighed.

"My heart goes out to you, Mary. Your story touches me deeply." Marvela thought awhile. "I think it's possible for a birth mother to get more information now, but I'm not sure what the rules are. They seem to vary from state to state. I promise to do some research and get back to you. Would you mind if I shared your story with Stan, so he could help me with the research?"

"I wouldn't mind. I have great respect for Stan, and I know he could be helpful to you. I would be so grateful for anything you could find out." Mary wiped her eyes and spoke haltingly. "I think you should know I wrote a note to the adoptive parents I asked nurse Barbara to deliver. I expressed my desire that the baby be named Angela. I have no idea if they got the note, or if the name was chosen. She would be more than sixty-five now.

Her birthday was May 20, 1942." She closed her eyes. "I have given up hope that I will see her, but I could die in peace if I knew she was OK." Mary held on to Marvela's hand.

Just then the hospice nurse bustled in. She nodded to Marvela and addressed Mary. "Time for your shot. Before I put you to bed, I'll give you a nice warm sponge bath. That should help you relax for the night."

Mary waved and managed a weak smile as Marvela left the apartment.

CHAPTER SEVENTEEN

When Marvela got back to her apartment, she called Stan. "Stan, I'm going to need your help on this one." She related Mary's story and asked him advice on how to proceed.

"I have a lawyer friend whose specialty is adoption laws, I'll ask his advice and get back to you," Stan responded.

The next evening at dinner Stan shared information his lawyer friend had given him. "The adult adoptee must give consent before the birth mother could contact her. So we need to find Mary's daughter as our first step."

"A giant first step, but not impossible," Marvela commented. "I have a hunch that the adoptive parents named the baby Angela. She would be around sixty-five, so she could have undergone several last name changes by now.

It took Marvela and Stan about a week of almost noninterrupted searching on the Internet before they hit pay dirt. Marvela came across a story in an online *Adoption Journal* submitted by an Angie Hensley-Black. In the story she related the circumstances of her adoption, something she found out after her parents died. She also expressed a desire to find her birth mother. It took Marvela awhile to track down more information about the author, but she found that Angie Hensley-Black lived in Ann Arbor, Michigan. There was no listing in the Ann Arbor phone book for an Angela Black, so Stan and Marvela started calling all of the Blacks in the Ann Arbor phone book. It took more than twenty-five calls before someone answered who knew an Angie Hensley-Black. The woman who answered said she had a sixth—grade teacher by that name.

"I was impressed that we shared the same last name," she said laughingly.

"Would you be able to give us her address or phone number?" Marvela inquired.

"I haven't seen her in years, but I think her husband's name was Ed or Ted."

Marvela found a Theodore Black in the phone book. A girlish voice answered her call.

"I am trying to contact Angie Hensley-Black. Could you help me?" Marvela asked.

"She's my grandmother. May I ask why you want to contact her."

Marvela decided to stay as close to the truth as possible. "My name is Marvela Higglesford. I live at *Forest Glen* Retirement Community in Johnson County, Kansas. I have a friend who is dying. She knew Angie as a child, and wants very much to contact her."

"Well, I'm not sure if I should do this. My grandmother is recently widowed and we try to protect her as much as possible. My dad should be home soon. I'll tell him about your call, and if he approves I'll give you her phone number."

"I'll be waiting for a call," Marvela responded warmly and gave her phone number.

At dinner that evening she and Stan talked about how best to proceed.

"First, we need to verify her identity to make sure she is indeed Mary's child," Stan said.

"No, the first step is to get her phone number," Marvela smiled and patted his hand.

After dinner Stan came to Marvela's apartment, hoping they would get a call. After waiting about an hour there was a call from Theodore Black, Angie's son. He was guardedly friendly, and wanted to know more about the dying friend.

"Just a minute, please." Marvela put her hand over the receiver and whispered the request to Stan.

Stan whispered back, "Tell the whole story after you get verification."

"I want to tell you the whole truth, sir, but first I need to know if Angie Hensley-Black is the person I am seeking. Is her name really Angela, and could you give me her age?"

"Her name is Angela, but she prefers Angie. She turned sixty-six on May 20. Now what is your story?" Ted asked rather curtly.

Marvela answered, keeping her tone friendly. "The dying friend is likely Angela's birth mother. Her name is Mary Vasser. She gave birth to a baby daughter May 20, 1942, at a home for unwed mothers in a suburb of Chicago. She knows the name of the adoptive family was Hensley."

There was a long pause before Theodore spoke. "My mother has expressed a wish to see her genetic mother, so I'm sure she would want to contact this woman. My father died rather suddenly two weeks ago, so my mother's state of mind is quite fragile. Hmm, if this woman is dying there may not be much time." Ted's voice became warmer.

"Do you think you could ask your mother what she would like to do?" Marvela ventured.

"Mother is strong-willed, and she would have trouble forgiving me if I didn't tell her." He thought awhile. "I'll go see her tomorrow and broach the subject as gently as I can."

"If your mother would contact Mary Vasser, it would make another mother very happy," Marvela said, her voice breaking.

The next morning Marvela received a call from Angie.

Her voice was tentative. "First, I want to thank you for your efforts to find me. How did you accomplish that?"

Marvela told about finding the article on the Internet and the many calls she made.

"You were certainly persistent," Angie replied with admiration. "I feel I can trust you. I will need your help in deciding how to proceed," Angie's voice grew stronger. "I would like to visit Mary Vasser, but I don't want to cause her undue stress."

"It might be best if I tell Mary about finding you," Marvela responded. "I could then ask her if she wants to see you, and call you back."

Angie gave Marvela her phone number and added. "Tell Mary I had a happy life, but I always felt something was missing." Her voice was tearful.

Marvela called Stan to inform him of the latest developments. "Would you like to go with me to see Mary today?"

Stan hesitated a second. "I don't want to intrude on the rapport you have established with Mary, but maybe I could be added support for you, and for Mary. I'll stay in the background."

"I'll call Mary and ask if we can come by this morning." Marvela made the call. Mary definitely wanted both of them to come.

Mary answered the doorbell, dressed in her robe. She was pale and her hair was tousled. "Please excuse my appearance. As you might guess, I didn't sleep well last night, even after I took a sleeping pill. Mavela, choose your seat, Stan brought his, and I have mine." She managed a faint smile. "The coffee is brewing if you would like some."

"Coffee sounds good," Stan responded.

"I'll get it," Marvela offered. "Your apartment is a mirror image of mine, so I know my way around. Do you take cream or sugar, Mary?"

"No coffee for me, it's forbidden, although I must admit I still have a weak cup every morning. Right now all I want is news of, of my daughter," her voice tapered off.

"That you shall have," Marvela said as she handed Stan his coffee, and pulled up a chair to face Mary. She reached for Mary's hand. "Angela wants to see you."

Mary started to sob, but soon gained control. "They did name her Angela! The name I've imagined all these years. Did you talk to her? What did she sound like? Is she happy? Does she really want to see me?"

Marvela took both of Mary's hands. "Yes, she really wants to see you. She said to tell you she has had a good life, but always felt something was missing. She evidently had loving parents and a devoted husband. At this time she is grieving because she just lost her husband."

Mary gasped, "Oh, the poor dear. Does she have children to comfort her?"

"I know she has at least one son and a granddaughter, since I talked to them. They are very protective of her. Of course there may be more children. I didn't question her about that. You will have a lot to talk about when she comes to see you." Marvela smiled.

"But when will that be? I-I probably don't have a lot more time left," Mary's voice faltered. She looked askance at Stan.

"Mary, from all I can gather, she will probably come as soon as travel arrangements can be made," Stan assured her.

Marvela nodded in agreement. "She mainly wanted to know if you were up to seeing her. I'll give you her number if you would like to call her?"

"Yes, yes I would like to do that. First I need to calm my nerves. I believe I will have that cup of coffee." She laughed and her face lit up.

Marvela brought her a cup of coffee and gave her Angela's number. "We'll leave now, so you can have a private conversation with Angela."

"I'm not sure what I'll say to her, or how, but I know it is up to me now." She grasped Marvela's hand. "How can I thank you?"

"The sound of your laughter was thanks enough. Keep us posted."

"We will take care of transportation, and anything else that's needed at this end," Stan added.

Marvela's phone rang the next morning before she got out of bed. It was Mary.

"She's coming, Marvela. I'll see her next week, only four days away." She sounded strong and vibrant.

"That's great, Mary. Do you have her flight schedule?"

"She'll get to KCI at 11:35 AM. She's left her return flight open-ended. Isn't that great?"

"Wonderful. I'll give this information to Stan. Do you want to go along to meet the plane?"

Mary thought a moment before replying, "I'd like to, but I'd better not. I want to save my energy for our visit."

"That makes sense, Mary. How did your first conversation go?"

"It was so easy to talk to her. We talked almost an hour. I had so many questions, and she answered very patiently. I had to hang up when the hospice nurse arrived. Angela assured me we would talk as long as I wanted when she was here."

"I'll go with Stan when he picks her up. Did you tell her to wear a red carnation?" Marvela chuckled.

"No, but I did ask her to describe herself. She's around five foot four, wears a size ten and has curly gray hair that used to be ash-blonde—like mine used to be."

"Do you have a picture of yourself at her age? Maybe there is a resemblance."

"There could be, although I was a little shorter and skinnier. I'll try to find one."

Marvela brought the picture with her to the airport. She had no trouble spotting Angela; she looked so much like Mary in the photograph.

When they arrived at Mary's apartment, Stan and Marvela stood inside the door and watched the teary-eyed reunion. Mary looked so energized. She had put on some makeup and wore a becoming blue blouse. After the initial hug, Angela stood back and looked fondly at Mary. "You are the missing piece in my life."

Marvela nodded to Stan. They left quietly.

Marvela asked Stan to come to her apartment for a celebratory drink.

"I know the sun hasn't gone down over the yardarm, but would you like a glass of wine?" Marvela asked Stan.

"By all means, we need to celebrate. This saga couldn't have turned out better, thanks to you, the angel of happy reunions."

"Speaking of reunions, Steve has invited me to his house for Thanksgiving. Ron and Marie can't make it, but I plan to spend a few days getting better acquainted with my grandchildren."

"I so regret not having children, so I could one day be a grandfather," Stan rued.

"It's possible I will have another grandchild," Marvela said happily. "Marie thinks she's pregnant. She is waiting for verification."

"Good news. I guess I envy you. Other than an aunt on my father's side whom I haven't seen in years, I have no family."

"You certainly have a lot of friends. We have called on several to help us, for which I'm deeply grateful."

"I've been fortunate to have good friends, but it's not like family. I don't spend the holidays with friends anymore. Most of them have established their own traditions."

"I plan to spend the Christmas holidays in England. Would you like to come along?" Marvela asked. She hid her crossed fingers.

"Are you serious?"

"Of course, Marie and Nigel would love having you. Can you get away for two weeks?"

"I'd move heaven and earth," Stan laughed.

Stan and Marvela had two wonderful weeks in England. Stan had been to England several times. He had once been an exchange teacher at a secondary school in Manchester, and he asked Marvela to travel there with him to look up a fellow teacher with whom he had kept in touch over the years. Christopher was now a widower who lived with his daughter.

"Stan, it is so good to see you," Christopher said from his wheelchair. "It looks like we have had some similar experiences." He chuckled as he glanced at Stan's wheelchair. Christopher had seriously injured his back in a fall from a horse. Stan told him about his accident. They shared anecdotes about being handicapped.

"What bothers you most, Stan?" Christopher inquired.

"Probably not being able to look people in the eye," Stan replied.

"I agree," Christopher said. "I have a lot more empathy for midgets," he laughed.

Marvela resolved to remember this conversation, and make more of an effort to speak to Stan at eye level.

They had a delightful two days with Christopher and his extended family. Several of Stan's former students came over to see Stan.

"I'm so pleased they remembered me," Stan told Marvela on their way back to Marie's.

"Stan, I'm not surprised," Marvela took his hand. "You're really quite memorable."

They looked forward to Christmas dinner with the Cramers. Marie told Marvela it would be a semidressy occasion. Marvela opted to wear white wool pants and a white silk-wool sweater embellished with seed pearl angels. It had been a gift from Sylvia, which she only wore on Christmas day.

When Marie saw her mother in it she exclaimed, "You look great, Mom! I hope that sweater never wears out."

"Wearing it has become my annual tribute to Aunt Sylvia," Marvela replied.

"And a fitting tribute it is." Marie hugged her mother.

As they drove up to the Cramer estate, they were in awe. Life-sized animated carolers dressed in authentic eighteenth century costumes greeted them singing "God Rest You Merry Gentlemen." There were tiny sparkling lights on all of the surrounding trees. As they entered the foyer a servant dressed as Father Christmas welcomed them. Iris had decorated the house in an eighteenth century motif. It was aglow with candles, including lit candles on two tall pine trees. The one in the library was decked out with old-fashioned ornaments. The white-flocked tree on the upstairs landing was a decorator's dream featuring golden miniature musical instruments, gold mesh bows, and sparkling rhinestone-studded ropes entwined around the tree.

Charles confided, "We have a sprinkler system, and there are fire extinguishers by each tree. How our ancestors kept their houses from burning down is a mystery to me."

"I don't think I would have the temerity to place lit candles on the trees, but it is so very beautiful," Marvela remarked.

Stan whispered in Marvela's ear, "So are you."

The dinner featured a standing rib roast decorated with Christmas ribbons, as well as countless side dishes including Yorkshire pudding. Desserts included plum pudding and Cherries Jubilee.

"Have the fire extinguishers ready," Charles quipped.

In a later conversation with Marie, Marvela confessed she couldn't help thinking about John's collapse when she was seated at the Cramer's table.

"I know the feeling, Mom. I still think of Dad when having dinner there, but the pain has lessened."

"It takes time, and understanding friends, doesn't it?" Marvela wiped a tear.

"You seemed to have found an understanding friend. Stan is great."

"He is really quite remarkable. Thank you so much for including him in all of the festivities. He's had a wonderful time." Marvela hugged her daughter.

Parting from her daughter was always a "sweet sorrow," but having Stan at her side was comforting.

CHAPTER EIGHTEEN

After they returned to *Forest Glen*, the weeks passed rapidly for Stan and Marvela. Stan spent several weeks at the NIT research center. He was able to stand for longer periods of time, although walking without rails to hold on was still not a reality.

Once again Jane asked for Marvela's help for the annual Valentine's dinner. This year the table decorations featured old-fashioned heart-shaped candy boxes.

"Three of them are authentic. I purloined them from three centenarians who are in nursing care. They gave me permission to use them, but probably can't remember doing it." Jane smiled and shook her head. "One of them is a real character. She always asks if she could dance for me. She then shuffles her feet and sings her version of the Hokey Pokey. I think she's a retired kindergarten teacher."

Marvela laughed. "One of the many characters I've met here."

"Speaking of characters, do you think we could get Leonard to lead all of the married men in 'Let Me Call You Sweetheart'? They could stand and sing it to their wives."

"I think Leonard would be honored. His voice is gravelly, but his timing is great," Marvela replied, "Trust him to ham it up."

The residents loved the dinner and entertainment. By popular request Marvela showed the power point featuring the lyrics of old love songs with appropriate illustrations for a sing-along.

After the dinner Jeanne remarked, "The singing improved by about ten decibel points."

"Yeah, I didn't have to turn up my hearing aides this year." Leonard chuckled.

The two couples went to the Pub after dinner for conversation and glasses of Bailey's Irish cream. Leonard got on his knees and sang "My Wild Irish Rose" to Jeanne. He then presented her with a long-stemmed red rose.

"Only one?" Jeanne laughed and kissed Leonard's bald spot. She knew that Stan had sent Marvela a dozen roses earlier that day.

"One for my one and only," Leonard replied as he laboriously got up from his knees.

Stan saw Marvela to her apartment. "You know you are my special valentine," he said as he kissed her goodnight.

The following morning Marvela vowed to spend more time with Della. They agreed to spend at least two days a week working out together. After the workouts, they would go to one of their apartments for coffee and snacks. They tried to eat healthy snacks, but indulged in pastries occasionally.

One day Della suggested they plan a World War II veteran's celebration for the fourth of July. With the help of Jane, and the approval of Kyle, they decided to have an outdoor picnic-barbecue. They would rent tables to be set up on the lawn. Luckily most of the tables could be set up in the shade. The kitchen staff would be enlisted to barbecue a variety of meats with the usual accompaniment of potato salad and baked beans, as well as trays of fresh fruits and vegetables. Entertainment would be provided by an over fifty-five jazz group, *The Jazzy Oldtimers.* The veterans were asked to wear uniforms, or any remnants they still had. Each would be introduced and asked to tell something about his/her war experiences.

The fourth was a hot Kansas day with plenty of sunshine. The residents were appreciative of the shade provided by large oak and maple trees. There was a lot of toe-tapping by the residents who thoroughly enjoyed the lively music. The honored veterans were applauded as they told stories of bravery and heroism.

"Another success," Stan told Marvela as they reviewed the day in her apartment. Marvela went over to Stan and kissed his cheek. "I want you to know how much I appreciate the support you give me in all of my endeavors. You are like a firm foundation to me."

Stan grasped her hand. "Marvela, is it a foundation upon which you'd consider building a future together?"

Marvela smiled. "I think this calls for a long discussion. I'll get some ice-cold lemonade, and we can talk."

Marvela set the lemonade glasses on the coffee table, and sat on the couch, tucking her legs under her. They sipped their drinks and were silent for several minutes.

Finally Marvela spoke huskily, "Stan, was that a proposal?"

Stan smiled broadly. "Yes, my dear, it was. I can't get down on my knees, but I'll rephrase the intent. Marvela, you have become the love of my life, will you marry me?"

Unbidden tears came to her eyes. "Stan, you have come to mean so much to me. It wouldn't be a stretch for me to say I love you." She reached over and took his hand. "Maybe marriage is another matter, or maybe not. Shall we realistically talk about the pros and cons?"

Stan frowned, and then forced a smile. "That makes sense, dear one. You probably want to talk about my physical limitations."

Her face fell. "Actually, your physical limitations are not a big concern for me. Are our age differences a concern for you?"

"Of course not," he said with near indignation.

"So we'll put those concerns aside," Marvela paused and took his hand. "May I ask what you want from marriage?"

Stan thought awhile. "I would be remiss if I didn't say I want physical closeness. I want to hold you through the night. Also the doctor tells me I am capable of making love." He gave a caustic laugh. "Of course that has to be proven."

Marvela half smiled. "I, too, would like physical closeness. But making love is so much more than a physical act."

Stan breathed a sigh of relief. "I agree wholeheartedly. I think we could create a whole new approach to the aesthetics of lovemaking." He reached out his arms to her and she went to sit on his lap. They kissed tentatively, then with passion.

Marvela found herself kissing Stan hungrily. "Am I getting too heavy?" she whispered.

"Never." He held her tight. "You're a perfect fit. I think our chemistry is OK." He nuzzled her neck.

"Is this what the kids call 'making out'?"

"Just a foretaste of things to come," Stan replied, kissing her soundly.

Marvela slid off his lap and went to sit on the couch. "Now for the nitty-gritty."

"Finances?" Stan offered.

"Yep."

"I've thought about that. We could make it simple by keeping our own bank and investment accounts." Stan waited for an answer.

"That might be best." She smiled. "I wouldn't have to change my name?"

"Not unless you want a simpler one," Stan laughed.

"A four letter word might be better." Marvela giggled.

"I know we'll figure out something that works for both of us," Stan said happily.

Marvela refilled their lemonade glasses. "Shall we drink a toast?"

Stan held up his glass. "To the most precious jewel I could find, her value is priceless."

As they touched glasses Marvela smiled, "Happiness is certainly not age relevant."

"Age is just a number," Stan murmured as he reached out and stroked her cheek. "Now I'd like to sit on the couch with you. If you'll move the coffee table a bit, I'll show you how I can maneuver my body."

"Your upper body strength is amazing," Marvela exclaimed as she watched him lift himself from the wheelchair onto the couch.

Stan put his arm around her. "This is better. Before I get any lewd ideas, I'd like to spend some time in intimate sharing. While you have shared some of your life experiences with me, there is so much more I'd like to know. Start from the beginning and tell me everything."

Marvela snuggled up to him. "I could say the same about you, but I'll start." She shared her experiences as an only child living in a small town in upstate New York. "My bout with polio made me become somewhat of a recluse in my elementary schoolyears. I had a home schoolteacher who did her best to make sure I kept up my studies. My mother tried to keep me socially stimulated by inviting girls my age to visit me. She was great about providing fun games and snacks to entice them to come. As a result I had some friends when I started attending school. I was a fairly good student, and not too rebellious." Marvela made a face. "I got into a little trouble with the high school administration when I wouldn't tattle on some friends who smoked in the bathroom. I also skipped school one day to be with a friend who was going to be sent away because she was pregnant."

"Always the champion of the underdog," Stan said as he hugged her.

"It must have been in my DNA because my parents were always taking in strays, be it animals or people."

"Your childhood sounds almost idyllic, despite your illness." Stan remarked. "Mine wasn't."

"I would like to hear about it, Stan." Marvela touched his cheek.

"My father had a drinking problem, although he wasn't abusive. Instead he'd withdraw to his room. He paid little attention to me. He'd get sober enough to go to work as a postal employee, but he didn't get the promotions he desired, so he was often sullen, even when he wasn't drinking. He had been good at sports, so I remember a few good times when he played ball with me. Mom was a dedicated school teacher who worked hard. She did her best to give me the attention I needed. She certainly gave me lots of love."

"Are your parents still living?" Marvela asked.

"My mother died at ninety of kidney failure. Unfortunately, I wasn't a match for a transplant, and she was too old to be on any list. She was amazing. She drove herself for dialysis treatments twice a week for three years until she was eighty-four. Her eyesight was failing, and she was getting weaker, so we had to place her in assisted living. She was mentally alert until the day she died, a great conversationalist, very well-read. As her eyesight failed, she checked out audio books from the weekly bookmobile. She stimulated my curiosity and intellect all of her life. I really miss her." Stan's eyes misted.

"I wish I could have met her. Were you able to see her quite often?"

"Yes, she lived in Independence, so I visited her at least once a week, or more. She loved eating out. We got to know most of the restaurants in the area quite well." Stan smiled as he remembered their good times.

"I often wonder how my parents would have aged," Marvela mused.

"If their daughter is any indication, they would have aged very well." Stan hugged her.

"You are sixty-nine, and I've celebrated seventy-five years. Are you sure that the age difference doesn't bother you at all?" Marvela queried, raising her eyebrows.

"What age difference?" Stan gave her arm a playful slap. "You told me once your biological age was sixty-seven. My biological age is undoubtedly in the seventies or more. Besides, I'll be seventy next month, so I'll be joining your chronological decade.

"Let's circle the date. We'll have to have a gala birthday celebration." Marvela picked up her calendar and looked at the notations penciled in for August. "It will have to be in New York. It's the day before Sid's wedding," she exclaimed.

"New York could offer a lot of intriguing options," Stan responded, "but I thought the wedding was to be sometime in June."

"She had set June 26, but her fiancé's mother died suddenly, so they set the date for August 15. Tyrone's mother was ninety-four, evidently quite spry, and looking forward to attending the wedding. Sid said she died in her sleep."

"A good way to go," Stan said. "Have you met Tyrone?"

"No, but if he lives up to Sid's description, he's quite a paragon." Marvela smiled.

"You do plan to accompany me, don't you?" She looked at Stan appealingly.

"I'll double check my calendar on those dates. I assume you would like to spend at least an additional week there."

"I would, if it's OK with you."

"I haven't been to New York since my accident. It will be interesting to see how they provide for the handicapped."

"Some hotels do a better job than others. I'll do some research, and see about booking—two rooms?" She asked mischievously.

Stan grinned. "Maybe we should start out with two."

The days before Sid's wedding were full for Marvela. She had to work on an expanded newsletter before the trip. The CEO had asked her to develop a publication he could use in their new marketing campaign. Marvela planned to use Sid's pictures of *Forest Glen* residents involved in a myriad of activities. She would include written descriptions of the range of enticing options available to members of the retirement community. The CEO hoped to attract new residents, but Marvela hoped that current residents, who preferred TV watching in their rooms, would be inspired to become more active.

She packed hurriedly the day before she would go to the airport with Stan. Sid and Tyrone met them at LaGuardia. After introductions and hugs Sid said, "You are staying at my place, aren't you?"

Marvela shook her head. "We have hotel rooms booked. No sense in overcrowding your place, Sid."

"We'll take you to the hotel. Tyrone has a minivan," Sid offered as she put her arm in Tyrone's.

"It will be my privilege," Tyrone smiled.

During the drive Sid's excitement was palpable. "We've decided to have the ceremony in a small Presbyterian chapel, so there will be about thirty close friends and family attending. I want you to be the matron of honor, Marvela. Tyrone's younger brother will be the best man."

"I'd be honored, Sid. You evidently changed your mind, the last I heard you were going to a justice of the peace," Marvela responded with surprise.

"Mother was a staunch Presbyterian, so it's a way of honoring her," Tyrone explained.

"Interesting, my grandparents were also staunch Presbyterians," Stan said.

"However, the ceremony will be quite untraditional," Sid said. "I plan to walk in on my daughter's arm, and we have written our vows in response to Tyrone's older brother Tom's questions. He's a spiritual director, a layman affiliated with the Jesuits, also an ordained Quaker minister." Sid beamed.

"I'd call that a real ecumenical ceremony," Stan commented.

Marvela leaned forward. "Sid, how formal is the dress? I may not have packed the proper clothes. I did bring the dress I wore to Marie's wedding."

"That will be perfect," Sid exclaimed. My daughter and I will wear knee-length jacket dresses. Mine is a shimmery cream-colored silk, and Lana's is sort of a silver silk shantung material. The men will wear dark business suits."

After Stan and Marvela got settled in their hotel rooms, Marvela knocked on Stan's door.

"If it's Marvela come in, the door is open."

Stan had changed into a dressing gown, and was seated in a comfortable overstuffed chair near the bed.

"You look relaxed. I hope I didn't disturb a nap."

"Oh no, although I will admit to being a bit tired."

"Shall we order room service for dinner?"

"You read my mind."

Over dinner Stan asked about Sid's family.

"Her parents aren't living, but a favorite aunt and uncle will be at the wedding, and of course her daughter Lana and husband Ahmed."

"Tell me about Ahmed."

"He's a medical doctor. His grandparents emigrated from Iran. He's a Muslim, but Sid says he's very interested in Christianity. Lana is a fairly devout Catholic, and she will raise her children Catholic."

Stan whistled, "I wasn't exaggerating when I used the word ecumenical."

After dinner and espresso they talked about the kind of wedding they would like.

"I think Jeanne and Leonard modeled an ideal *Forest Glen* wedding, could we do something similar?" Stan asked.

"With our own unique touches, of course," Marvela added.

"Of course, we don't have countless exuberant progeny to entertain the guests, so we'll have to be creative there." Stan laughed.

"I'll bet between us we'll come up with the perfect solution." Marvela went to sit on Stan's lap.

When Marvela started to draw away, Stan held her tightly. "Where are you going, love?"

"Tomorrow will be an eventful day. I want to help Lana all I can with any last minute preparations. And of course, we have to celebrate a very special event." Marvela tousled his hair and gave him a lingering kiss. "See you about eight in the morning." She got up and went toward the door, then looked back and asked tentatively, "Is there anything I can do for you?"

"I'm fine, sweetheart. Just keep me in your dreams." He threw her a kiss.

Before she went to bed, Marvela called the restaurant. "I would like room service to bring a deluxe breakfast for two at eight tomorrow morning."

She got up at six thirty, dressed hurriedly, and went to a nearby deli and party store. She bought an angel food cake, and found birthday decorations featuring the numeral seventy. She also picked up balloons, crepe paper streamers, and sparkling confetti before she made her heavily laden way back to the hotel.

At eight Marvela pushed the breakfast table, which now included the decorated cake as well as firmly attached balloons and streamers, to Stan's room. He was dressed, and in his wheelchair when he came to the door.

She switched on a cake server that played a raucous "happy birthday" as she pushed the breakfast table to the center of the room. She then lit seven candles on the cake, "One for each decade. Now make a wish before you blow them out," she instructed Stan.

Stan wheeled over to Marvela and took her hand. "My wish is no secret. I wish to make you as happy as you've made me." He pulled her down and kissed her. He blew out the candles on the cake while Marvela sang "happy birthday" in a clear soprano voice.

"As I've said before, you are indeed a marvel. There's no doubt this is my most enchanted birthday celebration, and you're the fairy godmother; one with a beautiful voice, which you've been hiding by the way," Stan said admiringly.

"I'm just lucky my voice didn't break. I haven't used it in so long. I sang in choral groups in high school and college. Other than lullabies to my children, I haven't used my singing voice since then."

"May I suggest that you exercise those vocal chords so you can sing lullabies to me." Stan grinned.

"For you I might just do that." Marvela reached for his hand and kissed it.

After breakfast they took a taxi to Sid's apartment where they helped Lana with the finishing touches on decorations for the reception tables. They were delicate pink, blue, and white carnations and baby's breath flower arrangements, featuring pictures from Sid's baby book on painted sticks.

"I know it looks like a baby shower, but Mom likes it," Lana explained. The place mats are cloud-shaped to sort of bring in something meteorological." She grinned.

Marvela laughed. "I think you have a lot of your mother's whimsy in you. The decorations are beautiful."

CHAPTER NINETEEN

Sid and Tyrone's wedding was certainly not traditional. Tyrone's brother Tom conducted an impressive ceremony. As he questioned the couple, he wove in inspirational homilies about love and marriage. In keeping with Quaker tradition, all of the guests signed a marriage certificate as witnesses.

Later Marvela whispered to Stan, "Let's incorporate that tradition into our wedding ceremony."

"I like the idea," Stan answered.

They spent the week after the wedding touring New York.

"I'd like to refresh my images of New York by taking a guided city tour, although this may seem redundant to you." Stan looked at Marvela questioningly.

"You know that sounds like a good idea. I know there are interesting sites here I've never visited," Marvela concurred. "But I do want to visit places where I worked. I'm hoping to see a few people who remember me," she added. "Some of my favorites were a lot younger than me, so they might still be around."

One of the producers with whom Marvela had worked closely invited Stan and Marvela to lunch. Laura was nearing retirement. While she had been active in international reporting, Laura was now working on human interest stories featuring a cross section of Americana. When Marvela described her current living choice, and some of the projects she had undertaken there, Laura became very interested.

"I plan to do a documentary on retirement options. We have an audience of Boomers who are rapidly becoming 'that age,'" Laura commented. "*Forest Glen* sounds like a place we should explore."

"I'm sure you would be welcomed. The CEO will love you. I will happily do whatever it takes to help," Marvela responded enthusiastically.

The week in New York was both exhilarating and exhausting for Marvela and Stan.

"I think we might have tried to do too much," Marvela commented when they got back to their hotel to start packing for their return trip.

"Although I enjoyed every minute, I'm ready for a slower pace," Stan agreed.

Before they went to their separate rooms, Stan pulled Marvela to him.

"I wanted to share a bed with you. I longed for you every night." He hesitated and swallowed before continuing. "I didn't insist, probably a lack of courage on my part, but also an old-fashioned and quite prudish feeling that the blessing of marriage would give me the courage to make love to you."

Marvela kissed him. "There is no doubt in my mind that everything will work out. Somehow this trip didn't seem like the time and place to me either." She grinned impishly. "And you know I'm no prude."

Stan returned her kiss with passion. "You are so right for me," he murmured. They left New York on different flights. Stan took a plane to Washington to meet his appointments at NIH. Marvela returned to *Forest Glen*.

Marvela called Marie as soon as she got to her apartment. Marie's due date was very near. Marvela got the answering machine, so she called Nigel's office. She figured it was around 10:00 AM in London. His secretary said he'd just arrived at the office—she'd buzz his phone.

He answered breathlessly, "Hi Marvela, so pleased you called. I just got back from the hospital. We have a beautiful baby girl! She was born at 1:00 AM. And guess what, we've named her Marvela, but we'll probably call her Vella, or maybe Marvel," he said elatedly. Marvela could hardly speak for the tears of joy, "I'm overwhelmed! How are they doing?"

"Marie was in labor for six hours. She was so brave. The baby weighs eight pounds, and is eighteen and one half inches long. She's adorable."

"Congratulations, Nigel, you'll be a wonderful father," Marvela said warmly. "Could you give me Marie's phone number, I can't wait to talk with her."

Marvela dialed the number with trembling fingers; Marie answered on the first ring.

"This is your mom, how is my namesake?" She tumbled over her words.

"Oh, Mom, she's so beautiful, not even red. She has a little tuft of black hair, and her eyes are blue. I so wish you could see her."

Marie went on to describe the baby in great detail. They talked for over an hour. Before she hung up Marvela told Marie she planned to fly to London as soon as she could make arrangements.

After unpacking, Marvela listened to the calls on her answering machine. One was from Leonard. His voice was choked with tears, and she had to listen carefully to understand him.

"It's, it's Jeanne. She's in the hospital in an unconscious state. Can you come?" Marvela felt devastated, but needed to know more, so she called the *Forest Glen* Health Services. She was told that Jeanne had been taken to the Kansas University Medical Center in an unconscious state two days ago. No one at *Forest Glen* had a recent update. Marvela called the hospital in an attempt to get some definitive information. They were unwilling to give her any details over the phone, since she wasn't a close relative. Marvela decided to go to the hospital to try to get firsthand information there. When she asked for the room number, she was told no visitors were allowed in Jeanne's room except immediate family.

"I'm a very close friend of Jeanne's. Her husband Leonard wants to talk with me. If I call the room, I'm sure he'll answer," Marvela pleaded. After she finally received the number, she called on her cell phone, Leonard answered in a barely audible voice "Leonard, its Marvela. I just returned from New York. I got your message on my answering machine. How is Jeanne?"

"Not good, she's been in and out of consciousness," his voice broke. They've got her on life support. "Marvela," he rasped. "She doesn't want that."

"May I come up?"

"By all means, we're in 482."

Marvela couldn't hold back her tears when she saw Jeanne hooked up to a respirator. She hugged Leonard, and they cried together for a while. She pulled up a chair and held Leonard's hand.

"I'm so sorry, dear friend. Can you tell me how this came about?" Marvela asked gently.

Leonard paused to gain control. "She'd complained of symptoms that sounded like pneumonia for several days. She coughed a lot, but thought home remedies would help her, so she wouldn't let me take her to the doctor." He shook his head and wiped his eyes.

So like Jeanne, Marvela thought.

Leonard blew his nose and continued. "Then she had a terrible coughing spell and collapsed in the kitchen, gasping for breath. I quickly punched our life support button. By the time help arrived she was unconscious, so the nurse called an ambulance. Oh, Marvela . . ." He sobbed. "She may not make it."

Marvela squeezed his hand. "But I think she will. At least we'll hold on to that thought."

Leonard stared into space. "I'm trying to, Marvela."

"Are her daughters coming?" Marvela wondered.

"Debra will drive in shortly from St Louis. The other two will fly in later tonight. They will be coming from California. Jeanine lives in Santa Barbara, and Suzanne lives in LA," Leonard could barely speak.

"How can I be helpful?" Marvela inquired.

He cleared his throat. "I've booked the guest room at *Forest Glen* for two of the daughters. Would you be able to put up the third one, possibly Debra?

"I would be most happy to have Debra stay with me, and I will provide transportation for all of them," Marvela assured him.

"Thanks, Marvela that would be very helpful." Leonard wiped his eyes before continuing. "Jeanne has a living will. If the doctor thinks she needs to stay on life support much longer, the girls and I will have to make a tough decision." His eyes filled with tears. "I want your input."

Marvela got up and hugged him. "I pray we won't have to make that decision. Jeanne is such a fighter. I have a strong feeling she'll make it," Marvela said with as much assurance as she could muster. She didn't want to give him false hope, but she believed strongly in the power of positive thought forms.

She kissed him on the cheek. "I'll go home now to get things ready for Debra. Call me when she arrives, and I will come to pick her up."

Leonard reached over to take her hands. "Thank you, dear friend," he said holding her hands.

When Marvela got back to her apartment she called Stan. First she told him about the new baby. Stan was delighted. Then she told him about Jeanne's condition.

"I am so very sorry," Stan responded gravely. "I should be home in two days to give my support."

When Marvela went to the hospital, she found Leonard and Debra bending over the respirator. Leonard's head was in the machine, and his ear was almost touching Jeanne's mouth. They straightened up when Marvela entered.

Debra went over to Marvela and hugged her. "Mom regained consciousness for a few minutes and was trying to tell us something. Leonard thinks she was protesting the machine. She was quite agitated, and she was moving her hands up and down."

Leonard looked up at Marvela. "She seems to be asleep now. Her breathing seems to be different than when she was unconscious. I've called for the head nurse."

The nurse came in and checked all of the indicators. "She could be breathing on her own, but the doctor will have to give the final word. I'll suction her breathing passages before I call the doctor."

"Couldn't we take her off of the respirator for a short time to see if she can breathe on her own?" Leonard looked pleadingly at the nurse.

"This is ultimately the family's decision, since the patient has requested that no extended life support be administered. The doctor ordered that she be placed on the respirator until she could breathe on her own, so he meant it as a temporary support system. I'll put in a call to him and ask his advice," the nurse responded.

After the nurse left, Leonard looked at the two women. "What do you think, girls?"

Debra took Jeanne's hand, "Mom, how about some input here." She was sure Jeanne gave her hand a slight squeeze. "It may be my imagination, but I think Mom is trying to tell us something."

"That wouldn't surprise me," Marvela said as she looked at Leonard. He nodded his head.

When the nurse returned she reported that the doctor gave his authorization to turn off the respirator for about two minutes to ascertain if Jeanne could breathe on her own. If she could, the time could be extended.

Three people held their breath as they watched the nurse pull the plug. Their eyes were glued to Jeanne's abdomen. When they saw it move there was silent jubilation.

Leonard looked at the nurse. "Let's try it for another five minutes. Shouldn't that indicate that she can breathe without being hooked to that thing?"

The nurse nodded. "I will again suction out any mucous. Of course I will have to check with the doctor before we take her off the respirator permanently." She treated Jeanne, and stood watchfully over her bed.

After five minutes with Jeanne still breathing on her own, the nurse left to call the doctor.

Jeanne's daughters Jeanine and Suzanne arrived soon after the nurse left the room. They had arrived at the airport on different flights scheduled close enough so they could share a taxi to the hospital. Debra went to the door to embrace them and share the good news about Jeanne's breathing.

Marvela hugged Jeanne's daughters and excused herself. "I'm sure the nurse will ask me to leave anyway, since I am not an immediate family member," she smiled at the sisters. "I'll go down to the cafeteria for a cup of coffee, and maybe a snack, since I missed dinner. I'll check in periodically. May I bring you something?"

"A cup of coffee, and maybe a sandwich, would be great," Leonard replied. "How about you, girls?"

"I'll come down later and bring up some hot tea, if you would like some," Debra asked her sisters.

"I would appreciate that," Jeanine spoke up. Suzanne agreed.

After about a half hour, Marvela went back to Jeanne's room carrying coffee and a sandwich for Leonard. She sensed excitement in the room.

"Mom opened her eyes and looked around. When she saw us she smiled and her lips moved," Jeanine said excitedly.

Debra added, "Then she drifted off to sleep.

"The nurse told us she could be taken off the respirator if she showed more signs of life," Suzanne chimed in.

Leonard's eyes were misty as he accepted the coffee and sandwich. "There's nothing like the energy of young people."

Jeanine, who was in her sixties, winked at her sisters. "I guess age is relative." She commented dryly.

Leonard looked at the women affectionately, "Anybody under seventy is young to me, and no one could argue that you girls brought a wave of energy to this room."

Debra kissed him before leaving to fetch the pot of tea. "I'll share a cup of tea with you, and then I'll be ready to hit the sack," she addressed her sisters. "I'm exhausted. I don't think I could have slept if Mom hadn't rallied, and I certainly don't want to be away too long."

When Debra returned, Leonard explained about the sleeping arrangements. "You girls go ahead and get some sleep. I'll get comfortable in this recliner and spend the night." After getting his assurance he would call if Jeanne's condition changed, the women agreed to leave for a few hours of sleep.

"I'll fix an early breakfast at my apartment for the three of you, and then I'll bring you back here. Would breakfast at six be about right?" Marvela queried. The women agreed, but Debra added, "I may not be dressed, but I'll try to make it."

"Our little sister couldn't get along without her beauty sleep," Jeanine teased.

When the women returned the next day, Leonard told them Jeanne seemed to murmur something unintelligible in her sleep.

"She is breathing normally, thank God. The nurse took the respirator away," he reported, a relieved look on his face.

Marvela told them she had some errands to run, but would be back to check on things around noon. She kissed Jeanne's forehead and left.

Jeanne's condition stayed about the same until evening. When Marvela came to pick up the sisters, Jeanne was speaking. She barely spoke above a whisper, so Leonard and her daughters hovered over the bed. "Do I have to be flat on my back before I get to see all of you at one time?" she whispered hoarsely, managing a smile.

Leonard looked up at Marvela and clasped his hands in a gesture of victory. "She's going to be all right." Just then the doctor came in on his nightly rounds.

"What have we here, a covey of beautiful women?" he joked. He took Jeanne's hand. "And you're the queen of miracles. They tell me you've been speaking to these handmaidens." He winked at Leonard.

Leonard nodded, "I think these girls gave Jeanne a shot of adrenalin."

Doctor Young looked around at the smiling women. "I should take you on the rounds with me, but first I'll have to ask you to leave the room while I examine the queen. Leonard you can stay if you like, but the room is a bit too crowded now."

Jeanine spoke, "We would like to hear your diagnosis and prognosis. We're unsure of why our mother collapsed."

"I'll meet you in the waiting room and give you a rundown," the doctor replied. "I will tell you that Jeanne's quick recovery did surprise me." He patted Jeanne's arm and smiled at her.

CHAPTER TWENTY

As they waited for the doctor, the sisters reminisced about the times Jeanne had surprised people with her courageous will. Marvela was an avid listener as she listened to stories of Jeanne she hadn't heard before.

"Dad was rarely home, so Mom had nearly all of the responsibility for our care," Suzanne commented.

"She not only cared for our physical needs, she was there for us emotionally. She read to us, and played with us." Jeanine wiped her eyes.

"And disciplined us," Debra added. "She didn't believe in spanking, but oh, that tone of voice when we displeased her."

"Like when you sneaked off to go ice-skating when she warned you that the ice wasn't safe," Jeanine said as she patted Debra's hand.

"And you fell through and nearly drowned," Suzanne chided.

"She was so sweet to me at the hospital," Debra remembered, "but when we got home, I got a lecture I'll never forget."

Doctor Young entered as Jeanine was saying with tears in her eyes, "Mom has always been there for us. I can't imagine life without her. I'm not ready to let go of her."

"I'm pleased to report that from all indications your mother will be around awhile," the doctor said as he smiled encouragingly at the women.

"That's great news," Debra responded. "Now for your expert opinion on what caused such severe symptoms. Was it a heart attack?"

"She didn't have a heart attack, or myocardial infraction, but she had many of the symptoms. Leonard said she complained of chest pains, nausea, and shortness of breath before she lost consciousness. He also reported that she had a bad cough and pneumonia-like symptoms for several days, therefore she had a great deal of congestion in her lungs, which she wasn't able to cough up. She lost consciousness because her body was rapidly being deprived of oxygen. It did put a strain on her heart, but we didn't find evidence of blood clots in her arteries. Her rapid recovery is probably due to her healthy lifestyle. Leonard said that her real age was seventy-two. I'm not sure what he meant," Dr. Young said with a quizzical look at the women.

Marvela spoke up, "Jeanne and I have taken the 'real age quiz' on the Internet. In essence you subtract years if you eat right, exercise, maintain a healthy weight, and have positive social relations."

Debra commented, "Mom is kind of a health nut. She had me take that quiz. Unfortunately my real age is older than my chronological age. But that should change now that I've quit smoking, eat healthier, and have cut back on alcohol intake."

"Good for you," Marvela said as she reached over and patted Debra's arm. The sisters nodded their agreement.

"Your mother has set a good example," Dr. Young addressed Debra, "keep up the good work. Changing bad habits is the best preventive measure we could advise."

The women went to Jeanne's room to say their good-byes before they left for the night. They took turns kissing Jeanne's cheek and telling her how much she was loved, and how proud they were of her. Tears flowed from Jeanne's eyes as she told her daughters how much they meant to her.

"You're the best medicine I could have," she said, trying to speak above a hoarse whisper.

Leonard walked with them to the lobby. "Good night, you covey of beautiful women." He chuckled. "I think both Jeanne and I will get some rest tonight."

Marvela checked her blinking answering machine when she got back to her apartment. Stan had left a message informing her that he would stop by the hospital when he returned the next day. Marvela decided not to call him back that night since it was so late.

Before leaving for the hospital the next morning, she called Stan's cell phone. "Stan, I can barely hear you over the hubbub. You must be at the airport."

"I am. In fact I'm boarding now. How is Jeanne?"

Marvela gave him the latest news of Jeanne's condition.

"You know, I guess I'm not really surprised at her rally. She's such a trouper," he said admiringly. "If all goes well I'll make it to the hospital close to dinnertime. I'll peek in on Jeanne, and then maybe we could go to dinner. I have something for you."

"I should be able to work that out. I will have to go back to the hospital to bring Jeanne's daughters back to *Forest Glen* where they're staying overnight."

When Stan came to pick up Marvela, Jeanne was propped up in bed eating gelatin. "Hey lady." Stan got as close to her bed as he could. "I heard you were at death's door, and here you are feeding your face."

Jeanne put down her spoon and leaned her head for a kiss. Stan complied, stretching as far as he could. She dropped her spoon and it clattered to the floor.

"Welcoming cymbals, Stan. It is so good to see you." She pursed her lips and made a kissing sound.

"How can I tell you how great it is to see you sitting up there eating," Stan smiled broadly. "Sorry to make you drop your feeding implement."

"I should thank you. I've never liked this awful wiggly stuff, but what can a hungry body do?" Jeanne laughed weakly.

"I'll get another spoon, Mom," Debra said. "If you're a good girl and eat it all, you might get something better next time."

"Leonard says my bossy daughter takes after me," Jeanne said as she looked lovingly at her husband.

"I can't tell you how I've missed your bossing," Leonard said as he crossed over to kiss Jeanne on the mouth. Debra came in with another spoon. "Hey, you two, it's dinnertime. You can smooch later."

"Speaking of dinner, I've asked Marvela to join me, if you can spare her for an hour or two." Before they left, Marvela told them the news of Marie's baby.

"New life," Jeanne smiled. "That's a lot to celebrate. Give Marie my love and approval when you next talk to her."

"We're also celebrating your new life." Marvela kissed Jeanne's cheek.

"Now you two be gone. There's a lot to . . . ," she cleared her throat, "discuss when there's a wedding in the offing." She waved her spoon at them.

Marvela shrugged and addressed the sisters, "What can I say, the queen has spoken. But be assured I'll come back for you."

As Stan and Marvela were driving to their favorite Greek bistro, where they could dine in near seclusion; Stan drove with one hand and reached over and took Marvela's hand in his. "I have some good news to share in addition to the surprise I mentioned."

"I'm quivering in anticipation," Marvela laughed. "Seriously, I hope the good news involves your physical progress."

"It does," he replied as he squeezed her hand. "Yesterday I was able to walk the length of the therapy room. Of course I had rails on either side to hold on to, but I was upright." His voice was shaking with excitement.

Marvela reached over and kissed his cheek. "That is good news. I'm so proud of you, darling. Are you going to divulge the surprise now?"

"No, that must wait until after we eat. I'm going to order the best wine in the house. After we finish a glass or two, I'll reveal the surprise. I'm not sure surprise is the right word, but it will have to do."

Both of them ordered moussaka, their favorite Greek dish. Marvela cleaned her plate, but Stan picked at his food.

"You aren't sick, are you, Stan?" Marvela asked with concern.

"No, just happily nervous," he replied cryptically.

He poured wine into their glasses. "I want to compose an appropriate toast for this occasion—too flowery may sound maudlin, but how else can I express my love for you."

They touched glasses. "Doubt thou the stars are fire, doubt that the sun doth move, doubt truth to be a liar, but never doubt my love," Stan quoted.

Marvela's eyes were shining with tears as she reached over the table and kissed him.

"I don't have a Shakespeare quote at the ready, so I'll respond with my truth." She took a deep breath. "I entrust my wholehearted love to your keeping. I know it will be safe there forever."

Stan withdrew a rhinestone-encrusted box from his coat pocket. "Your worth is greater than the most priceless jewels. But please accept this ring as a token of my love and commitment."

Marvela opened the box to reveal a two-carat blue sapphire ring circled by diamonds. "Oh, Stan, it's simply gorgeous. You know this is my favorite stone."

She crossed over to sit at his side, and they kissed, ignoring the waiter who came to present the check. He took one look and fled to the kitchen. The couple pulled apart, laughing.

Stan removed the sparkling ring from the box and placed it on Marvela's finger. "May this seal our betrothal." They kissed again.

The young waiter peeked out from the kitchen and turned to the chef. "I think that older couple just got engaged. I guess love is possible at any age."

The gray-haired chef laughed, "Don't you know age is just a number?"

Stan paid the bill and left a generous tip for the waiter. The chef stepped out of the kitchen. "May I offer my congratulations," he smiled and shook Stan's hand.

As they drove to the hospital, Stan mused. "I wasn't sure if giving you the ring at the restaurant was the right thing to do, but I think my instincts were rewarded," he chuckled.

Marvela admired her ring, "You could have given it to me in a busy subway, and it would have my undivided attention. I really should say *you* would have my undivided attention." She kissed his cheek.

Before she got out of the car, Stan returned her kiss with passion.

"I'll chauffeur Jeanne's daughters tomorrow. When I return, we can have a leisurely breakfast and maybe talk about a wedding date," Stan said as Marvela got out of the car.

Marvela kept her left hand in her pocket when she went to Jeanne's room to pick up the sisters. She would wait for a more appropriate time to reveal her engagement ring.

The next morning Stan met Marvela in the dining room for breakfast. Both of them brought their calendars.

"October is usually a lovely month climatewise in Kansas, but I'll need to check with my children before we set a definite date," Marvela said as she glanced at October dates.

"Shall we set a tentative date and then check with your children?" Stan suggested.

"My parents got married on October 4, that date has a lot of sentiment for me," Marvela circled the date, noting it was a Saturday.

"Sounds good to me," Stan agreed. "It can't be too soon." He mouthed a kiss.

"I'll admit I didn't think the second time around could be as exciting as this is turning out to be," Marvela said, her eyes shining.

"Come here, it's time to seal these decisions with a kiss," Stan said, opening his arms.

They didn't go back to the hospital until evening. Stan helped Marvela get caught up on the special edition newsletter. The deadline was a day away.

When they arrived at the hospital, they found Jeanne sitting up in bed and carrying on an animated conversation with her daughters.

Marvela went to the bed and kissed Jeanne on the forehead. Jeanne immediately spotted the sapphire ring. "Fourth finger, left hand, a gorgeous ring!" she exclaimed. "Have you set the date?" She hugged Marvela.

Marvela returned the hug. "Only tentatively until we hear from the kids."

Leonard went over to shake Stan's hand. "You're going to marry the second most wonderful woman in *Forest Glen*." He winked at Jeanne.

The sisters hugged the couple and offered their congratulations. "Would you like us to work up another dance routine for your reception?" Jeanine asked, chuckling.

"No kidding? That would be great," Marvela responded. Stan voiced his assent.

"We'd love an excuse to work on another routine, right, girls?" Suzanne looked at her sisters.

"Right, and I'd love an excuse to spend some time in California so we could rehearse." Debra winked.

On the way to *Forest Glen*, Suzanne asked Stan if he could give her and Jeanine a ride to the airport the next day. They had jobs to return to. Debra, who didn't work outside the home, would stay until Jeanne was able to return to *Forest Glen*.

Jeanne stayed in the hospital for three more days until she was released to the care of the nursing staff at *Forest Glen*.

Marvela and Stan brought her back in Stan's van. Leonard followed in his car. A *Forest Glen* nurse met the van with a wheelchair. Jeanne asked to wait in the lobby until Leonard came to wheel her to their apartment. Marvela, Stan, and Debra followed them with the many floral bouquets Jeanne had received at the hospital. Jeanne kept the roses Leonard had given her but asked Marvela to distribute the remaining flowers to residents of her choice.

"Would you stay and join me in a cup of Leonard's good coffee?" she asked Marvela and Stan. "The hospital brew was barely colored water."

"I've certainly been needing a cup of his java," Stan responded. "I don't know what he does to the coffee, but I can't match it."

"Nor can I," Marvela agreed, "and believe me I've tried."

"I'll keep making it as long as you'll come by to drink it," Leonard said. "Jeanne and I love your company."

They had a pleasant conversation for about fifteen minutes. Jeanne wanted to hear all about baby Marvela.

"You know how much I love bragging about the baby, but we don't want Jeanne to get too tired." Marvela rinsed out her cup and kissed Jeanne's forehead.

"You can rest assured we'll be back," Stan added as he wheeled over to kiss Jeanne's cheek.

Jeanne was wheelchair bound for three weeks before graduating to a walker. She came to visit Marvela one morning. They shared news about their families and happenings at *Forest Glen*.

After they had caught up on the latest events, Jeanne commented, "I'm getting bored, my brain cells need some stimulation. Any suggestions?"

Marvela thought awhile before replying, "Remember the time I suggested you and Leonard work up a comedy routine to present to the residents?"

"I do, but I thought you were joking."

"I wasn't. I think you two would be great and appreciated by people here who are probably bored as well. Live entertainment offers a stimulation that TV can never match."

"That's true. I'll talk to Leonard about it. I might be able to dig up some material from an over fifty drama group I once attended."

Leonard was willing to look at the material. Together they worked out some skits, which they tried out for Marvela and Stan. They performed a reading (dialogue-style) of George Carlin's views on aging as an example of the skits they had worked up.

L. Do you realize that the only time in our lives when we like to get old is when we're kids. If you're less than ten years old, you're so excited about aging that you think in fractions.

J. Yeah, you ask a kid, "How old are you?"

L. I'm four and a half!

J. You get into your teens, now they can't hold you back, "How old are you?"

L. "I'm gonna be sixteen!" You could be thirteen, but hey, you're gonna be sixteen!

J. And then the greatest day of your life . . . You become twenty-one.

L. Even the words sound like a ceremony. YOU BECOME twenty-one. YESSSS!

J. But then you turn thirty.

L. Oooohh, what happened there? Makes you sound like bad milk. He TURNED, we had to throw him out.

J. There's no fun now, you're just a sour dumpling. What's wrong? What changed?

L. You BECOME twenty-one, you TURN thirty. then you're PUSHING forty.

J. Whoa! Put on the brakes.

L. Before you know it, you REACH fifty, and your dreams are gone.

J. But wait! You MAKE it to sixty. You didn't think you would.

L. So you BECOME twenty-one, TURN thirty, PUSH forty, REACH fifty and MAKE it to sixty.

J. You've built up so much speed that you HIT seventy! After that, it's a day-by-day thing; you HIT Wednesday.

L. You get into your eighties and every day is a complete cycle. You HIT lunch, you TURN four thirty. You REACH bedtime.

J. And it doesn't end there. Into the nineties you start going backward, "I was just ninety-two."

L. Then a strange thing happens. If you make it over one hundred, you become a little kid again.

J. I'm one hundred and a half!

L. J. May we all make it to a healthy one hundred and a half!

Stan and Marvela laughed until tears came to their eyes.

"You two are great," Marvela exclaimed.

"Your audience will love you," Stan added.

"Now our problem is an overabundance of good material. We'd like you to help us choose the best," Jeanne asked.

"Jeanne insists we memorize the stuff. My brain cells will rebel if there's too much to learn," Leonard groaned.

"Whenever you're ready, we'll ask Kyle to put the act on the calendar," Marvela said. "You guys are really funny."

CHAPTER TWENTY-ONE

After the couple left, Stan and Marvela talked seriously about their marriage plans.

"Come closer, my love. I need some physical reassurance." Stan pulled her on his lap.

After a few minutes of kissing and embracing, Marvela pulled away and gazed lovingly at Stan. "Do we really want a formal wedding? Maybe we should just make do with a quickie wedding and get on with our lives."

Stan hugged her tightly. "Suits me."

"However, I have some breaking news," Marvela said excitedly. "Jan, the marketing director, called me this morning and asked if we might be interested in moving to a townhome on the *Forest Glen* campus. Seems there is a two-bedroom with basement vacancy. What do you think?" Marvela questioned.

"That is good news. I like the idea a lot. We would have room for all of our furniture and definitely feel more independent. Are you up to cooking?" Stan chuckled.

"I would enjoy fixing some of my specialties for you, my dear. We could also explore some of the fine dining in town. Do you think we can swing it financially?"

"I think so. I have a small inheritance from one of my uncles that I could invest in a sizable down payment. I'll talk to Jan about the particulars," Stan replied.

"What a godsend. After that down payment, the monthly payments would undoubtedly be less than our rent here, including those exorbitant maintenance fees." Marvela wrinkled her nose and added, "Of course I will contribute half of the monthly payments."

"Let's do it," Stan said enthusiastically.

"This calls for a celebration. How about going to the nearest espresso bar for lattes?"

"My treat." Stan grinned.

"Maybe we should call Jan and tell her we want that townhouse," Marvela suggested.

"Better yet, let's stop by her office before we go out for coffee."

They went over the details with Jan and signed the first papers. After they ordered lattes, Marvela remarked, "Was that an inspired decision, or what?"

"I really feel we made the right decision. Now the quickie marriage plans." Stan reached for her hand.

"I just had another inspiration," Marvela said, eyes alight.

"Let's hear it."

"Why don't we move into the townhome, get it fixed up to our liking, and then have the wedding ceremony there." Marvela paused to gauge Stan's reaction.

He squeezed her hand, and tears formed in his eyes. "That is an inspiring idea," he assured her.

Marvela continued enthusiastically, "We could invite about twenty or so of our closest friends. Hopefully that will include all of my children. Maybe we could find a Quaker minister to marry us, and everyone could sign a marriage document like at Sid's wedding." She continued breathlessly, "We could have a catered sit-down dinner."

"Jan gave me keys to the townhome. Shall we go look it over to get a better idea of the size?" Stan queried.

Marvela grabbed her purse. "Let's go."

After going through the townhome, they decided it would be ideal for their wedding plans if they kept the guest list small. There was a large living/dining area that could accommodate at least twenty guests.

"To make it easier on us, we could probably rent tables and chairs and possibly wedding decorations from the catering company," Stan suggested.

"Actually, we could wait to move most of our things until after the wedding, so there would be room for the seating of guests," Marvela added.

"I wonder how much lead time it will take to get your children here," Stan mused.

"I'll call them this evening and tell them we have to get married as soon as possible," Marvela laughed.

As soon as she returned to her apartment, Marvela called Steve, Ron, and Marie. "You're invited, no commanded, to attend my wedding to Stan," she told them. "Saturday, October 4 is the preferred date."

They agreed to check their calendars and do everything they could to attend on that date.

Marie reminded her mother she would have to travel with a two-month-old baby she was breast-feeding.

"A baby I can't wait to see. I would have flown to England after her birth if Jeanne hadn't been in the hospital," Marvela lamented.

"You called me every day, and I was able to send you cell phone pictures, so you weren't entirely bereft," Marie reminded her.

"As soon as we get settled after the wedding, Stan and I plan to spend several weeks with you, if you'll have us."

"That would be very special. I want you to bond with your namesake." Marie's voice was gleeful.

Steve arranged for a week's vacation with Sonia and the children. They would spend a few days in Colorado after the wedding. Luckily Ron was able to arrange a stopover on his way to a meeting in Washington.

Marvela was elated that all of her children and grandchildren could attend the wedding on the date she had chosen. She shared the good news with Stan at dinner. They ordered sherbet for dessert and took it to Marvela's apartment to enjoy while they finalized wedding plans.

"We'll have to call catering companies first thing in the morning. Keep your fingers crossed, this will be a short notice," Marvela said as she looked through the Yellow Pages.

Stan helped her make a list of things she should ask the caterer.

Marvela started calling at eight in the morning. Fortunately, the third catering company she called had a cancellation on October 4. They agreed to furnish tables, chairs, and linens for twenty-four people. After conferring with Stan, she called them back with their menu preferences. The caterers referred Marvela to a decorator who specialized in wedding decor.

"I think we're all set. It may cost us an arm and leg, but it will be worth it," Marvela told Stan with a satisfied grin.

Marvela conferred with a member of the writing group who attended an unprogrammed Quaker meeting. He recommended an ordained Quaker minister who didn't have a congregation since he chose to attend the traditional silent meeting.

Stan suggested that he and Marvela attend the Quaker meeting the next Sunday to meet this minister and discuss plans for the ceremony.

Sitting in silence until two members of the group of about twenty felt led to speak was a new experience for Marvela and Stan. They met with Dorlan, the minister, after the meeting. He gave them a pamphlet that told some of the history of the Quakers.

"We will read it with great interest," Stan commented. "I really enjoyed the quiet time and felt the two speakers had relevant observations. Social justice is a prominent topic, I gather."

"It is. Quakers, or Friends as we're called, have a long and inspiring history of working for just social action," Dorlan replied.

They told Dorlan they wanted a Quaker-type wedding document in which the wedding guests would sign their names as witnesses to the marriage. He offered several suggestions for the ceremony, which would basically be similar to the queries Sid's brother had used at her wedding.

On the way back to *Forest Glen* they went over the wedding plans.

"It's coming together very well," Marvela remarked. "There's one more important detail. What am I going to wear? What is your favorite color, Stan?"

"I like deep rose, or maybe coral is the right term," he responded.

"I shall look for a dress of that shade," Marvela smiled. "I'm glad you didn't choose turquoise." She giggled.

Marvela asked Jeanne to go shopping with her. Jeanne was getting around well using a rhinestone-studded cane.

They spent several hours one morning going through racks of size 8 dresses.

"I'm afraid I'm wearing you out, Jeanne. Finding the right dress in a coral color has proven to be more difficult than I thought it would be," Marvela said wearily.

"Let's make one more stop at a small dress shop in the Plaza," Jeanne suggested. "Debra found an exquisite cocktail dress there. I have a feeling we'll find the right dress at that place." Jeanne's intuition proved correct.

When they described what they were looking for, the woman waiting on them said, "I think I have just the dress." She brought out a silk-wool dress with a shawl collar and a softly flaring midcalf skirt in a shade she called autumn pink.

Marvela modeled it for Jeanne.

"You've found the perfect coral dress. You look beautiful in that color," Jeanne enthused.

That night Marvela and Stan made out the guest list.

"Do you think we could squeeze in thirty people?" Marvela ran her fingers through her hair. "I don't want any hurt feelings. Who can we leave out?"

Stan thought awhile. "Maybe we should arrange another reception for all of the residents," Stan suggested and grinned. "That is after we get back from our honeymoon."

"That's an excellent idea!" Marvela exclaimed. "We could ask the kitchen to bake some decorated sheet cakes and make some punch. By the way, where are we going for our honeymoon? Are we really going to have one?" She looked at Stan, eyes sparkling.

"Of course, I wouldn't forget something that important." Stan chuckled. "Would I?"

"I can't believe we haven't discussed it?" Marvela marveled.

"I'd like to take you to Costa Rica. Have you ever been there?"

"I've always wanted to go. They say it's a poor man's Hawaii."

"I know an airline pilot who lives in San José. He has invited me to come any number of times. I'll fax him and ask if he'll help make arrangements. How does a week at a deluxe hotel in Costa Rica sound?"

Marvela kissed him. "More than I could have dreamed of."

The weeks before the wedding passed rapidly. Marvela got out an issue of *New Horizons* and partially finished a second one. Leonard and Jeanne would finish it while she and Stan were on their honeymoon. Arrangements were made with Kyle for the residents' reception, which would take place a week after the couple got back from their honeymoon.

"I'll have it coincide with one of our better musical entertainments. I think the management would spring for the cake and punch," Kyle told them. "After all, you do for us, it's a small thing to ask."

It rained steadily the week before the wedding.

"I guess the rain won't hurt our parade," Marvela remarked to Stan, "but of course, I would welcome the sun."

"You will always be my sunshine, but drier weather would certainly make life easier for the decorator and caterers, not to mention picking up guests," Stan said as he looked out at the pelting rain.

The rain let up, though the skies were cloudy the day before the wedding when they were to go to the airport to pick up Marie and the baby. Marvela was so excited she had trouble dressing. She had to put on her blouse the second time because it was inside out the first time; she fumbled with the buttons on her jacket. She wasn't satisfied with her makeup, so she wiped it off with cleansing cream.

Stan was waiting for her in the living room. "Hon, we'd better get going," he called.

"I'm coming, dear." she grabbed her purse and earrings. "I'll put on my makeup in the car. I'm so eager to see that baby, I'm just beside myself," she laughed.

Stan let Marvela out at the terminal gate. Marie and Vella had just disembarked and were on their way to the baggage claim.

Marie handed the baby to her mother. Much to Marvela's amazement, the baby snuggled on her shoulder without making a sound. She held her all of the way back to *Forest Glen*.

"Marie, sorry I didn't greet you properly. I guess you were upstaged," Marvela said as she gazed at the baby adoringly. "She's just as beautiful as you described. The pictures didn't do her justice."

"No problem, I've become used to being upstaged." Marie laughed. "Nigel hardly has eyes for me anymore. Well, not as long as Vella is around. I will admit he has been wonderful to me."

The baby fell asleep in Marvela's arms. When they got to the apartment, she was placed in a crib Marvela had rented.

"I've arranged for a reliable babysitter to watch Vella during the wedding. I'm just sorry that my time with her will be so short," Marvela said regretfully.

"We're expecting you and Stan for a long visit after the wedding. Now may I have that hug."

Mother and daughter hugged and did a little dance around the room.

Marie sang, "If you're happy and you know it, stomp your feet."

"You two are a little crazy, but I love it," Stan remarked. "I'm off to the airport to pick up Steve and family. Ron will catch the shuttle and a taxi later."

The family had a late dinner in the private dining room. Marvela ate very little since she was too intent on holding the baby. She only gave her up when it was time for Marie to feed her.

Steve's children had brought gifts for the baby. Susan wondered why Vella didn't reach for her bright new rattle.

All-wise Andrew answered, "Silly, she isn't old enough. Maybe in a few more months she will be."

"But look, her eyes are following it," Marvela said.

"She's probably per . . . precocious," Andrew announced, proud of his vocabulary.

"She undoubtedly is," Steve agreed and winked at Marie.

Ron and Stan watched wistfully. Both were wishing they had children.

Marvela had arranged for all of her children to stay overnight at *Forest Glen*. Ron, Marie, and the baby would stay with her. It was fortunate that

Betty's furnished apartment was available while she visited her family; so Steve, Sonia, and children had comfortable sleeping arrangements. Sid and Tyrone would be flying in the morning of the wedding and flying back the day after. Marvela was delighted Sid would be there, but she was concerned about the expense for such a short visit. Sid reassured her that being there was worth any monetary cost.

CHAPTER TWENTY-TWO

The day of the wedding started out rainy, but the sun came out in the afternoon. It turned out to be a lovely day. Kansas weather was usually at its best in October. The family, along with Sid and Tyrone, enjoyed a brunch buffet hosted by Jane and Della in the private dining room. Marie urged her mother to nap in the afternoon. She lay down for a while when Vella slept but couldn't fall asleep. She wanted to spend as much time as possible with her family.

About four that afternoon, Stan reported that all was in readiness at the townhouse. White-damask-covered tables seating four had been set up. The decorator had picked up the color theme of autumn pink. She found roses of that shade, so bouquets of coral tea roses graced each table along with white candles. Baskets of pink-hued gladioli surrounded the small "stage area," which was set apart by white latticework interwoven with vines. Marvela and Stan would sit on white wicker chairs during the ceremony, and the minister would stand to one side as he conversed with the couple.

They had finally settled on twenty guests to be seated at five tables—the space limit for tables since there had to be room for the "stage" and the string trio. Stan chose to wear a navy blue suit and a coral-colored silk tie, which Leonard and Jeanne found after scouring countless shops.

The couple was radiant as they greeted the guests. Stan was able to stand by, holding on to his wheelchair. All were enchanted by the beauty and ambience of the setting.

As the four-course meal was served by three of the young waiters from the dining room, Marvela looked around at the guests. She was delighted to see her four special women friends enjoying each other's company. Della, Jane, Gina, and Bubbles were chatting animatedly. Leonard's laughter dominated the table he shared with Jeanne, daughter Debra, and Dorlan. Jeanne's daughters Suzanne and Jeanine were unable to come. *There wouldn't have been room for dancing anyway,* Marvela thought.

At another table Andrew kept up a constant chatter, while Susan looked around wide—eyed. Sonia was lovely in a robin egg blue gown, and Steve looked distinguished in a gray pin-striped suit, which set off his wavy silver hair. It was hard for Marvela to believe that he was over fifty. Where had the time gone?

Ron and Marie sat with Sid and Tyrone. Ever-youthful Sid looked gorgeous in a strapless, floor-length emerald green gown. Her dangling emerald earrings were a wedding gift from Tyrone. She told Marvela she would probably be overdressed for the occasion, but so be it. Marie chose a flattering red knit suit. Her center-parted dark hair was long and shiny. Marvela thought she didn't look a day over twenty-five. Ron had a flattering shorter haircut and had grown a becoming mustache. He just returned from a working vacation in southern California, so he looked tanned and fit. Marvela beamed at her handsome children.

Gerald, the *Forest Glen* CEO, and his wife shared a table with Kyle and his wife Kimberly. Since Marvela didn't know Gerald very well and had never met his wife, she was reluctant to include them on the shortlist of guests. But Stan had been a classmate of Gerald's at Kansas University, and they were nominal friends; so there was an obligation. His wife was very heavy and looked uncomfortable in a too-tight floral-patterned dress. Kyle and his vivacious wife, dressed tastefully in an off-white suit, seemed to keep the conversation flowing.

Marvela regretted they weren't able to invite more of their friends, but she was pleased there would be a reception for all of the residents later. She thought about the two years and one month or so that she resided at *Forest Glen*. She couldn't help feeling some pride at her accomplishments but was humbled by the thought of the friends who had supported her. She thought fleetingly of John and the life they might have had. Would it have worked out? Then she glanced at Stan. If there were really soul mates, he had to be hers.

After coffee was served, Marvela and Stan excused themselves to freshen up while a string trio of *Forest Glen* residents played a medley of love songs. When they played *Intermezzo*, Marvela and Stan entered. Stan easily swung himself into one of the wicker chairs, while Marvela and the minister took their places. The minister proceeded with the queries. He asked Marvela and Stan to relate the values they shared and the qualities they would evidence as husband and wife. With the help of two canes placed by his chair, Stan pulled himself to a standing position. Marvela stood and faced him as they recited their wedding vows.

"I vow to be your loving husband. I will cherish you with all my heart for all the days of my life." Stan's eyes were adoring.

"And I vow to be your loving wife. I will cherish you with all my heart for all the days of my life." Marvela's voice was shaky but strong.

"I now pronounce you man and wife," Dorlan intoned.

The guests rose to a standing ovation as Stan reached over to kiss Marvela.

The couple then took their seats and exchanged simple gold wedding bands.

Dorlan took the wedding certificate to each table for the guests to sign. As the document was passed around, Kyle's wife Kimberly, an accomplished vocalist, sang the wedding song "Because," accompanied by the string trio. "Because you come to me with naught save love . . . a wider world of hope and joy I see . . ."

Champagne was served, and a designated party at each table proposed a toast. Leonard's toast provoked laughter and tears.

"I rise to offer a toast to my dear friends. May this day be the beginning of a new chapter in a love story that will endure forever. Marvela and Stan, you have brought us much joy and happiness. May it be repaid a hundredfold. You have shown wisdom and good taste in your selection of one another. You also evidenced wisdom and good taste in your selection of Jeanne and me as friends." He paused when the audience laughed. "May you love as long as you live, and live as long as you love—wherever that may be."

Leonard's toast was followed by Steve, Bubbles, Kyle, and Sid. Steve spoke for his siblings. He listed the wonderful qualities Marvela evidenced as a mother and welcomed Stan to the family.

"May we call you Dad?"

Stan nodded and clapped.

Bubbles's toast was in rhyme.

She came to us one fortuitous day.
How we did without her, I cannot say.
She and Stan, a formidable pair,
Give unstintingly and always share
Their talents and gifts to help those in need.
They are friends in spirit and always in deed.
We wish them the happiness they well deserve.

She made an abbreviated Charleston move and curtsied to the couple.

"I better quit now, or I'll lose my nerve."

The audience applauded and several shouted bravo.

Kyle was next. "I can't top that, so I'll just say, Marvela and Stan, please accept our deepest gratitude for all that you have contributed to *Forest Glen*. We hope that we will be graced by your contributions for many years to come. May God bless and keep you."

When Sid rose to speak, the audience gave a collective gasp; she looked so beautiful.

"I won't try to match Leonard or Bubbles in originality," she smiled at them. "I have collected some friendship quotes that remind me of my wonderful friend, Marvela. Stan, I have no doubt that you, too, will become a great friend. I'll begin with a quote from Walter Winchell. 'A friend is one who walks in when others walk out.' Len Wein said, 'A friend is someone who is there for you when he'd rather be anywhere else.' I can't give credit to the authors of the following quotes, the Internet simply said Anon. 'A friend is someone who knows the song in your heart and can sing it back to you when you have forgotten the words.'" She looked at Marvela and smiled, "You always seem to know the words." Marvela threw her a kiss. "And lastly, Marvela believed in me when I ceased believing in myself. 'Friends are God's way of taking care of us.'"

Marvela dabbed at her eyes while her friends applauded.

It was midnight before the last guest departed. Marvela was reluctant to say good-bye to her children and Sid. There were tears, but mostly laughter and hugs. The couple retired to the bedroom—the only room they had furnished so far.

They spent that night embracing and reliving the momentous events of the evening. It was so satisfying to lie in each other's arms. The consummation of their marriage would wait until they were relaxing in Costa Rica.

They had an idyllic week in Costa Rica, reveling in the cool mountain sunshine and enjoying languid boat trips to the warmer beaches. They spent an overnight at a Quaker-run lodge in Monte Verde. There, American Quakers helped the locals make and sell cheese. Stan and Marvela followed a path in a nearby cloud forest until the going got too rough for Stan to maneuver. They visited a coffee plantation and sampled the delicious Costa Rican coffee. In San José they bought handmade souvenirs for their friends. Stan's pilot friend, Miguel, and wife, Rosetta, joined them for dinner at the Grand Hotel, followed by a concert in the newly renovated state-run palace of the arts.

They were impressed by this beautiful Central American country. Although there was evidence of poverty, it wasn't as pervasive as the poorer countries surrounding it. They saw some armed guards, but Costa Rica didn't support a military force.

"As a result, there is more funding available for health care," Miguel informed them proudly.

As they bade farewell to their new friends, they expressed a desire to return to this fascinating country.

When they returned from their honeymoon, the couple found all of their furniture had been moved to the townhome. They smelled coffee brewing.

"It could only be Leonard's," Stan remarked as he wheeled his way into the kitchen.

Jeanne rushed over to hug Marvela. "You look wonderful. I assume the honeymoon was all you could ask for?" Jeanne winked.

"All and more." Marvela winked back.

Printed in the United States
151665LV00002B/67/P